The Chosen

By

MaryKay Duffy

ISBN: 1-4033-7923-8 (e-book)
ISBN: 1-4033-7924-6 (Paperback)

Library of Congress Control Number: 2002094721

This book is printed on acid free paper.

Printed in the United States of America
Bloomington, IN

United States Copyright Office

1stBooks – rev. 01/20/03

This book is dedicated to all of the heroines and heros making this world a better place everyday through their acts of bravery, kindness and compassion.

Acknowledgements

This book is a testament to persistence. Along that path I have many people to thank for their help and support. First of all I would like to thank my family for their input as I continued to write and rewrite the book.

I would like to thank my editors, Henri Forget, Dianne Wiroll and my son Joseph for their wonderful suggestions, caring and consideration of this work.

Thanks to Deb Barrett of ViewSpirit.com as she was the gifted artist that designed the cover for this book and I hope its beauty will be of inspiration to the readers.

I have so many wonderful friends and colleagues who have been beacons of enlightenment along my journey to complete this work, you know who you are, many thanks to you.

To my clients who even as I coach them, always teach me valuable lessons about life, thank you.

To my husband for supporting the space in our lives for this book to come to fruition.

Introduction

This book was created to inspire hope and celebrate the success of the work of all of the people that seek to support the universe in a positive way in their lives.

I have used some fiction and some non fiction to create a story about human strengths and frailties, metaphysical mysteries, divine intervention, miracles, love and a message around the criticality of the power of positive thought and the continuity of life.

I hope this book speaks to you in a way that encourages your unique contribution to humanity whatever you choose that to be.

Blessed Be.

Table of Contents

Chapter One. The Pharaoh's Revenge...

She looked around the room wondering which direction the sounds were coming from. The loud crashing sounds seemed to grow closer. Shanta tried to lift her head from the floor. Her eyes blurred from pain and the effort to concentrate. She allowed her head to rest on the floor again trying to remember why the crashing sound was so familiar. Guards, the shields that the guards carried. Of course, that was the sound. Slowly she began to recall. Her eyes blurred again, this time from the pain of memory. Tears began to flow from her eyes, streaking down her young face. Recollection of her mother's slaughter assaulted her senses. Then, she wondered...

Why was I not slain as well?

Shanta began to review the recent events as her mind cleared. She recalled the death of the Pharaoh, and now his younger brother was in power. The new Pharaoh had made no secret of his distaste for the old religion and all of its followers.

Why did he not order me put to death? What could he be planning?

MaryKay Duffy

Shanta was the high priestess of her group, and yet everyone else in the group had been murdered, and she was still alive. She began to recall her mother's instructions...

"To find the answers you seek, you must relax and let your thoughts turn inward."

It was hard for Shanta to do this under such distress and with so much sorrow in her heart. She was so unhappy because of the deaths she had witnessed. She felt alone, in pain and frightened of the future. She recalled that her duty as her mother, Tiy had instructed her, was to survive in order to lead. Mother had predicted adversity, unlike any they had ever known. Shanta realized now why her mother had been so hard on her during her training and suddenly she reminded herself she had to focus her thoughts, and calm herself.

Her mind recalled the process. She had learned this during her training. She began to slow her mind and relax her muscles. She knew she had to find out more about what had happened. She let her thoughts begin to drift. Her body soon joined her thoughts. As her astral journey began, she saw much destruction as she floated through the palace rooms, searching for survivors.

2

It was horrifying: The temples were destroyed, hundreds murdered, blood was everywhere. Then she saw him, the new Pharaoh. She drew close. He was talking with two men. She listened. Shanta was sickened by what she heard of his plans.

What had this man been afraid of? Why was his goal to destroy the Order?

His concept of control was so simple in his mind, yet so wrong in a cosmic sense. But for him, this would soon prove fatal.

Did he imagine that these murders had freed him from his destiny?

She listened as he discussed the future, his plans for her torture, her slaughter, the removal of all her limbs, to be thrown in pieces to the crowds.

"A public display must be made to frighten the people."

She heard him say.

"This sect and its followers must never survive. Once she is dead, that will be accomplished."

Shanta now understood why she was spared from that initial slaughter. Her demise would be his public spectacle, his demonstration, and illustrative of what he perceived as control over this spiritual group.

Shanta worked to subdue her heightened emotions. Her body and mind had to remain stabilized, calm. She realized she had to intervene. To do so would require her complete concentration. The Order had to go on. Her life must continue, until the predicted time of her passing. She had seen her time of passing. Mother had shown it to her so she would be ready when it came. But this was not the time, so she was free to protect, whatever the cost, herself and the Order. Shanta looked closely at the face of this murderer. He had ordered the death so many of the most gifted from the order. She looked at his face, so young like hers, but unlike her he was ignorant and cruel. She drew close, for none of the three could see her, as her astral body was beyond their view. She reached out with her small hand, and pushed it through his linen robe. She reached through the cloth, through the flesh and grasped his heart. She felt the small veins separate, and then she tugged quickly and pulled away. She felt no sorrow as she watched his face contort in pain. She knew he would die. Shanta watched as

4

other two men tried to assist their new Pharaoh, however she had no need to remain, knowing their efforts to be futile. She had to go; there was work to do.

Shanta was back in her room, having completed her astral journey. Now, she knew she had to escape.

To the mountains, yes, she would have to go to the mountains. Now how to get out? Shanta had grown up in this palace. There were some well-guarded secrets and hidden exits. The huge pillars that lined the palace had small sections of space several feet under them and they lined all of the main corridors in the palace. Tiy must have seen this time coming, because she had instructed Shanta at a very early age about the secrecy of what she referred to as the *tunnels*.

Shanta remembered sitting on her mother's lap. The robe her mother wore was silk and very soft to the touch, with such wonderful colors. Her face was very beautiful.

The memory was so comforting and suddenly Shanta felt her body grow warm. She realized Tiy's spirit was with her. Shanta was so happy, and yet she realized her mother's presence was here because she was in danger of some kind. She went to the portal, tapped at the marble slab. On the left, in the middle, then the slab shifted slightly. Shanta pulled at the opening, and the panel moved.

She slid down under the marble slab, and then as she left, pulled it back over head. Pushing up she heard it shift firmly back into place. She began to crawl forward. Quickly and quietly she moved down the dusty, dark corridor. It was hot and narrow and seemed endless. She felt lost and more alone then she had ever been. Shanta turned the corner; finally, the space was somewhat larger. She realized she must be under the main living quarters, and she could hear loud sounds: shouting, confusion resulting from the Pharaoh's death. She began to become frightened because she realized these sounds were familiar to her. She recognized them yes, this would be her time of death. She felt the pain in her ankle, and looked for the last time at the site of her own demise. Tiy had shown this to her years before. Death would be swift. She now knew why mother's spirit had come back to stay with her, because it was time. The snake's poison was almost instantaneous in its effect. Her last thoughts were swirling in her mind, mother, the order, survival, but it was becoming so dark.

Chapter Two. Adrienne's Awareness

Expands...

Adrienne opened her eyes. Dr. Hart was saying something to her. Dr. Hart's mouth was moving, but Adrienne could not understand. She was scared, and her heart was racing.

"Adrienne, you are safe; relax you are back."

Adrienne just stared at the doctor's face, his white hair framing piercing blue eyes. It was a face she began to remember. She just stared at him, for what seemed to be a long time, and then she spoke.

"Doctor, I feel so weak, unsettled."

"Adrienne, you have been on a very long mental journey. Your hypnosis session has ended. You are back now, so sleep if you wish. I will sit with you for as long as you rest, and later we will talk about what happened."

She looked up at the face she knew so well, and her eyes grew heavy, then she drifted into a deep sleep.

When she awoke, the first thing she noticed was that the lab in Dr. Hart's office was filled with sunshine. Adrienne could hear the singing of birds outside the lab. She felt so relaxed; what a lovely day! She really felt good, and she was anxious to finish her meeting with Dr. Hart today. She knew he would be able to answer a lot of the questions she had been wondering about for a long time when they reviewed the contents of the tapes from today's hypnosis session.

Dr. Hart and his staff had been working with Adrienne for months. Adrienne had been introduced to Dr. Hart by her family physician. She had been having some problems sleeping and her doctor thought hypnotherapy would help her. She had immediately liked Dr. Hart when she met him, he had very kind eyes and a very caring manner which she found comforting. Dr. Hart had worked in the field of psychology and hypnotherapy for many years.

His experiences with some clients had led him to do a great deal of work in past life regression, using a variety of hypnosis techniques. Working with Adrienne, he had discovered that she had psychic tendencies which they found fascinating. At that point, Adrienne had begun to work on her psychic abilities, to increase the strength and awareness of what she could do. In the past, Adrienne always believed her thoughts, or "trips" as she called them as a child, were just vivid daydreams. Dr. Hart had helped her to understand that she was actually visiting these places using her astral body. She was surprised to discover all the things she could do. Dr. Hart helped her to not be afraid of her gifts, and to develop them, not to shut them out because of fear.

As she began to move her head a bit, she saw Dr. Hart sitting close by.

"Dr. Hart, thanks for sitting with me while I rested. I feel so much more like myself; the rest really helped me. What else are we scheduled for today?"

Dr. Hart replied, "Today, we are working on transcribing the tapes from today's session. We are at the point that we need to review your most recent regression. Since the transcription will take some time, and we have already done some regression work today, you could finish up now and we could start again tomorrow. Adrienne agreed that worked well for her, she was looking forward to spending some time in the fresh air. Dr. Hart began to walk Adrienne to the door, and then said, "Oh, I forgot to tell you, I've also contacted a young colleague of mine, Professor Hans Ergine, he will be coming tomorrow to talk with us about the work your doing with past life regression. He has written several books on the subject and I think will be very helpful due to his experience and interest in this field."

Adrienne nodded, and then said goodbye to Dr. Hart and left to enjoy the rest of the afternoon.

The next day, as Adrienne walked the length of the corridor with Dr. Hart she wondered how her life had become so complicated. In retrospect, she began to realize the complexity was not new. Reflecting on her childhood, she always knew she was different. Her mother understood to some degree that she was unusual. Adrienne recalled her mother's face the day she stared into her eyes and commented on what an old spirit she was.

"Age that was far beyond her years. Wisdom and knowledge that was much older than she knew".

Mother had special talents also, but her tendencies would drift to the negative on many occasions. Adrienne had learned many lives ago she was not to go to the dark side for help. She had seen her mother wish harm on people, and rely on evil deities to help her with some of her psychic battles. Over the years, she could see her Mother had changed for the worse because of this. Adrienne seemed to innately sense that the price for asking for help from this source would ultimately lead to servitude of the basest nature.

"Adrienne, shall we begin?" The voice startled Adrienne from her thoughts.

"Oh, Dr. Hart, I was lost in thought; yes, let's begin".

She looked around the room. It was so clinical, white tiles, chrome tables, yet somehow the sense of order and familiarity made her feel secure. She knew Dr. Hart was leading her through an important clarification process that, while confusing for her, was preferable to the mire of thoughts and experiences she previously had dealt with on her own.

Professor Ergine walked into the room. Adrienne felt an immediate sense of familiarity somehow in being around this man. He was in his thirties, blond hair and blue eyes, she was trying to recall when or where she might have met him. He looked at her and said nothing, and then he walked closer and stared. Hans felt as though he knew this woman, as though they had been close in some way, but he could not make the mental connection to where or when he may have known her. He found this annoying because normally he had excellent recall.

Dr. Hart's voice interrupted his thoughts.

"Professor Ergine, have you met Adrienne? I thought this was your first time meeting, but you seem to know one another. Professor? Hans?"

Moments passed, Hans turned, a bit startled. Hans was embarrassed that he had been so distracted in his thinking about where he might have know Adrienne from, he felt sure he had met her.

"Dr. Hart, yes, yes, of course. I guess my thoughts were just drifting for moment; excuse my rudeness."

Dr. Hart began speaking again.

"Well, Professor Hans Ergine, meet Adrienne Raines."

They both nodded and shook hands, and they seemed to speak in unison, "It's a pleasure to meet you."

Adrienne and Hans both chuckled in response to their mild embarrassment. Dr. Hart interrupted the moment.

"Well, Adrienne, are you ready?"

"Yes," she said," Doctor, let's begin."

Dr. Hart walked with Adrienne into a smaller room. The room was painted in pale, subtle colors. The room was shaded, excluding much of the daylight. The chair was modern in its design. It seemed to be structured or shaped for the human form. Dr. Hart explained to Adrienne that she would recline in the chair, and he would put up side supports so that she would be protected from falling. Then he would play some tapes. Her job was just to relax and listen. Dr. Hart finished by explaining that, "Professor Ergine will monitor the taping and take notes. When the initial part of the session is complete he may request one or two additional points of historical clarification. These points would be then become the focus of the next hypnotic regression session."

Dr. Hart asked Adrienne if she understood the procedure. Adrienne nodded, to let him know she was clear on what they were going to be doing. Dr. Hart then pulled the most recent tape from his pocket.

"Adrienne, I am now going to begin the session, are you ready?"

Adrienne contemplated the question; her honest response was, no. She had never been ready for any of this. She was however always aware of having been a little different from other people. As the years had unfolded, she continually discovered a constant variety and complexity of these differences. She finally got to the point of needing to understand as much about what was happening to her as possible. Still, she was never ready for the confusion these regression experiences brought about, but she was ready to try and make sense of as much of the past as she could.

So let's begin, she said to herself,

and then to Dr. Hart, she said

"Yes, I am ready; let's begin."

Adrienne listened as the tape of her previous regression session played. Hans began to take notes, the same notes that he would eventually use to research the validity of the historical data that was mentioned. Adrienne knew the data was valid because she had been there. But, for the scientific community more specific proof was required. Dr. Hart was helping her to sort this experience out. Dr. Hart was also working with her to help her manage the emotional impact of being able to recall these past life experiences. Adrienne considered it fortunate she had found Dr. Hart to help her work through this experience. She hated to think of what it would have been like to try and work through these issues alone. The all listened intently to the account of the slaughter of innocent victims, the death of the Pharaoh, the escape, her death. The tapes stopped. Dr. Hart was the first to speak.

"Adrienne, how do you feel?"

"I'm always a bit nervous after we do a session."

Hans looked at Adrienne, and he wondered if he should ask his questions now, or wait. He decided to wait, as she did look a little pale. Dr. Hart spoke again.

"Adrienne, let's have you rest here for a few more minutes; I will call my office and have some sandwiches ordered. When we have had some time to relax, and something to eat, then we can decide whether to continue today or start again tomorrow."

Adrienne nodded, and closed her eyes. When Dr. Hart left the room, Hans began to collect his notes, putting them into his usual methodical order. He reflected, as he collected his papers, that the order in which he worked was always the same. He liked having his files in chronological order, it helped him to process his thoughts clearly from the day's work.

He could not help thinking about how disconcerting it would be for him if he had thoughts from another life existence popping in and out of his thinking as Adrienne did. He was sure he would find that emotionally upsetting.

How did she maintain her sanity?

He wondered. Well, if she were working with Dr. Hart that would explain, to some degree, how she was coping with all of this. Dr. Hart was world renowned for working with complex cases such as this. With that reputation, and his years of experience working with these techniques, he had helped many people. He also worked with a team of seasoned colleagues that worked with Dr. Hart's clients as they learned to manage all of the new feelings that occurred during such intense work.

Having collected all of his things, Hans glanced over at Adrienne. She lay still, as he looked at her, and he pondered the task before him. Always the skeptic, his position had to be more in the role of devil's advocate. He was seeking cold, hard, reliable, verifiable facts. If the case could not be substantiated beyond any doubt it would not be included in his book. She seemed sincere, but appearances can be deceiving. He had learned that for certain. He began to think back to his earliest years in research, remembering some of the cases that did not hold up under his scrutiny. He had learned then, that the surface appearance of things was not enough to assume authenticity.

Dr. Hart entered the room, his white coat stiffly scratching the door as he rapidly moved past the doorway.

"Adrienne," he spoke very quietly.

Adrienne's eyes opened, her color had improved.

"Do you feel up to having lunch now?"

"Yes, doctor, let's go."

The trio slowly left the room and walked the length of the corridor without speaking. The Lunch was brief, but revitalizing. Dr. Hart could see Adrienne's energy was still low, therefore he insisted the rest of the day's activities be rescheduled for the next day. Dr. Hart felt that Adrienne needed the rest. While Adrienne spent some time away from the work, Dr. Hart would look over the notes from their work together and think about how they should proceed in the process. Hans was leaving the lab as well, so Dr. Hart asked Hans to drive Adrienne home. She gratefully accepted. Despite her prior denial, she felt drained. Listening to one's own death experience, even in a past lifetime, was emotionally unsettling. They walked from the stately research building, continuing down the path toward the parking lot. The trees were ruffled by a slight breeze. Multicolored flowers lined the path, and birds chirped as though it was the first sunny day they had experienced.

Hans glanced at Adrienne, as they walked. She was really lovely, and somehow he was not intimidated by her beauty, instead he felt a sort of inexplicable familiarity.

The sun reflected on her blonde hair, as it flowed in the wind. He felt that it was fate that had led him to this project, and this work. But more importantly to have met this woman whom he felt so drawn to. He agreed with the singing birds. This was a most wonderful day.

The car was hot when they first opened, the doors. Hans opened the windows, and then turned on the air conditioner. The forest green sports car was really hot, having captured some of the sun's intensity. He addressed Adrienne.

"It usually takes a few minutes for the car to cool off".

The intensity of the heat really brought Adrienne back to the present, and distracted her a bit from her anxiety following her session today. She finally said,

"I don't mind, really."

Adrienne stared out the window. As they pulled away from the building, she wondered if she should be doing this regression work. It was more draining than she had thought it would be. She reminded herself of the more than unsettling string of events that brought her here to work with these people. Years of seeing images that others did not see. Having knowledge of things before they occurred. So many things, so many years and she had only confided in a few people about what was happening. Her mother seemed to understand, to some small degree. It seemed mother had some level of special abilities herself, and Adrienne knew that. At the same time, she also understood that her mother was incapable of the things that she could do. Adrienne kept many things secret which at times, she herself couldn't believe. Well, more accurately, she didn't want to believe them. She was quite skeptical of the things she experienced. In her desperation to ignore these personal revelations, she had trained herself to ignore them whenever possible.

As they drove along in silence, Adrienne told herself to stop thinking about all this. This was a protective habit she had developed, and as she thought about trying to forget everything, for now at least, she was reminded of Dr. Hart's training. Dr. Hart had encouraged her to not be afraid of her thoughts, to review them, and consider the relationship of the thoughts or impressions, to each other. He encouraged her to discuss those perspectives with him whenever possible. His approach was now part of her clarification process. She realized that the tapes today did relate in many ways to other occurrences that she had experienced. Tomorrow she would discuss this with the doctor. She would work with him in his way and not avoid the progress any more.

Han's voice startled her.

"Penny for your thoughts?"

Adrienne refocused on the moment. She looked at Hans.

"What did you say?"

"I said, penny for your thoughts. You seemed so far away. What were you thinking about?"

"Oh nothing, just daydreaming I guess."

Hans sensed a slight hesitation to answer his question. He decided to see if he could understand what the resistance was about. He inquired further.

"Daydreaming about what?"

Adrienne thought for a second and decided like everyone else, he would think her slightly mad if the she told him about what she thought about, or daydreamed about. Dr. Hart was her first official confidant and she was just learning to trust him. For now, she decided her thoughts would remain confidential. When Adrienne spoke to Hans, she decided to try and keep her comments fairly superficial in nature.

"Oh the weather, the day is really lovely".

Hans responded, "Adrienne for someone enjoying the day so thoroughly you still seem slightly pale and somewhat worried."

She looked at him, realizing they would be working together on this project with Dr. Hart, she decided to share some of her thoughts.

"I am still adjusting to the facts of my death. The time has past, but the occurrence is one that never completely left me on some emotional level. Hearing the specifics is still quite a shock. The emotional impact of the violence and the sad endings are very unsettling for me."

She surprised herself, sharing such a candid response, but somehow it seemed normal to be discussing this with him.

"Adrienne, why are you going through all this?"

She looked at Hans wondering why he was asking so many questions about her work with Dr. Hart. She simultaneously realized that her emotions were based on fear rather than concern.

Adrienne had developed an ingrained concern when it came to questions and answers relating to this aspect of her life. Adrienne said, "I just realized I am not sure how to address you? What do you prefer to be called?"

Hans realized he felt so comfortable with her he was asking her a lot of questions for two people who had just recently met, and then he responded, "Please call me Hans".

"OK, sounds good."

Adrienne responded. She then continued to answer his question.

"Hans, it is really simple. I needed help in understanding all the aspects of my life and personality. Dr. Hart has been assisting me, through his more experienced approach, in clarifying my past as well as current existence."

Hans realized as she spoke, she was still really tired out from the day's events. He decided that he was letting his desire for knowledge blind him to the fact that Adrienne was in no state of mind for questions regarding the day's events.

"I'm sorry for all the questions. I'm being thoughtless. Your day has been tiring. You must excuse me. Will you?"

Adrienne responded,

"Yes, of course, let's forget it".

Adrienne looked at Hans, and she realized that he meant her no harm. Her intuition about people was quite accurate. She had been using it since childhood. Growing up so self sufficiently, her intuition had been quite a help in surviving in a major city, considering the many people she had encountered. Some were very good, and some were quite cruel. She realized that she was now getting close to home.

"Hans, my place is at 700 Montaro Boulevard, it's three blocks straight down from this exit".

Adrienne pointed to her building, as they pulled up to the curb.

The property looked over the ocean. Adrienne loved her home. It was the first place that she had ever owned in this lifetime. She had purchased her condominium with an inheritance from her aunt. She enjoyed seeing the familiar sight through the windshield, as the car approached her driveway.

"Hans, I appreciate the ride. You were really kind to drive me home."

Hans glanced over saying, "Well, I enjoyed spending some time with you. Dr. Hart has requested I sit in on tomorrow's review session. I need to get a specific time period in history documented for my research. So, it appears we will be seeing each other tomorrow. I look forward to seeing you then, have a good night."

Adrienne stepped out of the car and said, "OK, Hans, I will see you tomorrow."

Adrienne ran up the steps keys in hand. It was very warm outside. She looked forward to the coolness of the condo. She opened the door to the entrance hall and felt relief from the air conditioning. She went to the kitchen quickly opening the refrigerator door and pulled out a cold bottle of soda. Filling a large glass with ice, she began to anticipate the refreshing relief. She felt much better at home, more relaxed. She pulled off her shoes and walked to the balcony. Sipping her drink, she relaxed in her most comfortable chair and looked out at the ocean. The sun shimmered across the water, like thousands of small gold coins reflecting across blue-green crests of water. She marveled at this beautiful creation. The beauty and the practicality of nature were one of her basic loves in life. She looked up at the sun. It was so omnipotent. Present since the origins of time and here until the end of time in this universe. All things are relative, all things continue. She had written chants and prayers to the sun that had come to her before. Words lovely and profound yet from a time long past. They were so impressive. She could not believe she could have created them. Dr. Hart had helped her to realize the old religions had many profound belief systems, prayers and rituals. He had collected as much of this data as possible and saved it over many years. Adrienne found out that her recollections were prayers learned as a child in another time. He helped her recall so much information. Identifying origins of all of these facts was her current endeavor. She felt tired, the ocean air had really relaxed her. Sleep was definitely a good idea. The tension of such a confusing day had left her feeling exhausted. She began to walk to her bedroom and then she realized she had forgotten to check the mail. She grabbed the key from the shelf. Opening her front door she went to the mailbox and unlocked it.

She quickly pulled the mail out and shut the mailbox door. She did not really want to end up chatting with a neighbor today. As she dropped the envelopes on the table she noticed the edge of a handwritten letter sticking out from the rest. The writing was familiar. She pulled the letter out and opened it. As she read the note, in her brother's handwriting, she learned that his religious retreat at the seminary was ending in three days. She was so happy for him, and as she read on she felt even better. His time away obviously had been successful. He was coming home to be with her for a while. What good news this was. She put the letter down and decided, for now, there would be no more interruptions. Then she went off to sleep.

Chapter Three. Valley of the Pharaoh's...

The next day, Dr. Hart, Adrienne and Hans sat at the circular table in the lab. Papers, audio and video tapes, books and notes were piled all about leaving hardly any free space. Hans looked at Adrienne saying, "From the information Dr. Hart and I have reviewed so far we've narrowed the site to Karnak or Thebes. Karnak was a great center of living for at least fifty Pharaohs. Thebes was also a popular central area for religious celebration. The order you were trained by appears to have been very well established. We will need a few more specifics about the order, their habits, and any other related facts we can obtain. Once we have that, we can get a specific geographical location."

Dr. Hart looked at Adrienne and said,

"If we are going to try to get more information, we should proceed with another regression today. Adrienne, how do you feel about that?"

Adrienne did not hesitate replying, "Yes, we should definitely do it today. I am anxious to move as quickly as we can."

Dr. Hart rose from his chair saying,

"I will get the lab ready. Can you meet me in twenty minutes?"

Adrienne nodded saying,

"I just need to make a quick phone call, and then I will walk to the lab."

Dr. Hart left the room. His footsteps echoed down the hall. Hans spoke, "Adrienne, do you mind if I am present for the session?"

Hesitating for a few minutes, she slowly responded.

"Hans, I am okay with you attending the session but only if you agree to keep this completely confidential. Until we have completed all of the pieces to this work, and I have personally reconciled with all of the ramifications, I want to keep all of this very quiet"

She arose from the table pulling a few pages together. She began folding her notes and putting them away. Hans joined her in collecting his books and notes realizing that he was really excited that he could be part of this experience.

Adrienne and Hans decided to walk together to meet Dr. Hart at his office. Adrienne was anxious about the session, hoping that some information that would help their progress would be forthcoming. She realized she was nervous about Hans being present. Up to now most of her work had been exclusively with Dr. Hart. She knew Hans could help in the work, but still felt a bit shy about him being involved. Adrienne approached the door to the office and decided she did not want to start a session feeling nervous. She intuitively knew there was nothing to worry about, and therefore decided to stop reviewing negative possibilities in her mind. As she opened the door, she reminded herself to trust in the universe.

Chapter Four. Shanta's Ceremony...

Shanta was aware of a strong scent.

What was it?

She looked upon the statues in front of her. She was actually at the center of this grouping of statues. The closest and largest image of them had very few carved features and seemed very old. As she looked at the statue more closely she could see it was a representation of both male and female combined in unisexual form. Something very sweet-smelling was burning in a large and ornate incense tray placed in front of the main statue. There were voices chanting constantly, the sound rising and falling in a monotone rhythm. Shanta felt some confusion. The chanting and the smoke from the incense were hypnotic. Shanta could see two women walking toward her. Their bodies reflecting through their gowns. As they approached her, they gently grasped each of her arms and she began to walk with them. They were leading her up a small stairway that had been built behind the main statue. The same statue that she had been staring at so intently. As she passed through the shadowed passageway, she could see ancient symbols of some kind etched in the back base of the statue. However she could not see clearly enough to read them. Shanta began to realize that her vision in general was blurry. The stairs she was climbing seemed so very high. They seemed to be going up so much higher than she thought possible. Finally, the three women entered a room completely carved from stone. There were no windows and beautiful ornate drapes lined the walls. The drapes had embroidered pictures of men and women dressed in great finery, participating in celebration. There had been a panel added at the end and Shanta was stunned to see the embroidered work featured a woman who could have been her twin. As she looked closer, she realized it was in fact her image.

The two women began to dress her placing a large, heavy crown upon her head. They gave her instructions as they removed her linen dress and wrapped her in a shimmering garment.

"When you hear the crowd's cheers, raise your arms straight up and do not move, we will do the rest."

Shanta slowly nodded in agreement. She was hardly aware of what was happening.

She was mesmerized by the beauty of the golden threads of the material, as they wrapped the skirt around her waist. A large golden pin just below her navel held the garment firmly around her hips. The pin was fashioned in a shape like the sun. It felt heavy on the lightly spun linen and gold skirt. She was nude under her diaphanous skirt, and from the waist up. The two maidens rubbed red powder on the nipples of her breasts and dark charcoal on her eyes, quickly putting the finishing touches on their priestess. Slipping shoes with golden and deep blue inlay on her feet and finally her necklace of sapphire, gold, and emerald. Shanta now saw only flashes or shades and the colors seemed so beautiful. The women continued to speak, she could understand what they said, but everything seemed so slow, somewhat distant, as though it were all happening to someone else. Suddenly, the stone slab of a door in front of her seemed to disappear. She felt the women hold her arms in order to bring her forward to another room with a shiny marble floor. They continued to walk her farther onto a large platform. Then suddenly there was such a loud sound, and she was exposed to bright light. She was blinded by the sun's rays. It had been so dark in the other room. Now, her vision blurred, she tried to clear her eyes to see if she could identify the roaring sound. There were flower petals all over the outdoor platform where she now stood. The sun felt hot on her skin. Her eyes finally cleared somewhat, and she was beginning to see some shapes.

"Shanta",

She heard the two women call her name in a loud, hissing way.

"Your arms"

She dimly recalled their instructions. She slowly lifted both arms. Now she could see clearly. There were people everywhere; so many people shouting, chanting.

Her mother had told her this day would come, now she understood what was happening.

Why hadn't they told her it was today?

Then she remembered. Mother had always told her that the first day of public initiation was frequently held from the chosen, and now she could see why. The anticipation of appearing before such a huge crowd of people would have made Shanta very nervous. Thousands of people were shouting; she could not believe Thebes had so many people. Her arms ached and she did not know how long she had been there.

Suddenly she was aware of her mother's presence. The crowd hushed and Tiy's voice echoed as she spoke.

"The day has come. She who was sent is ready. As the stars have foretold, it is the day, the hour, and her father's rays embrace her. This day is the first; from this day the most powerful speaks through Shanta. As it has been from the beginning of our time, so it will continue."

The crowd began to shout Shanta's name and cheer in unison. Her mother's voice spoke out again.

"Let the festival begin."

Chairs were brought out on the platform. Large chairs that were covered with carvings of the sun, and scenes of many of life's daily activities that take place under the blessings of the sun god. Shanta was escorted to the largest chair in the center. She watched with a somewhat clearer mind as people broke into groups depending on their preference for the festival's activities. Her headpiece was so heavy, she dared not move.

Small groups had broken into performing rituals that seemed to involve everything from chanting, frenzied twirling and dancing, music, candles, incense, and more. This celebration of the people's adoration of the sun and what it meant to their lives would continue until dawn. However she welcomed the sunset on this day. It was then that her handmaidens escorted her from the front of the temple, back inside to her chambers. Her mother waited while Shanta was dressed then they walked together, alone for the first time.

"Mother, why did you not tell me it was my day?"

Tiy responded, "I wanted to make it of no concern or worry to you, Shanta. That is why you were given the herb tea. It was meant to dull your mind. It is over now, no other festival will ever be as the first. Shanta, you must sleep now. We will talk about these things more tomorrow."

Shanta lay down on her bed. She was very tired and quickly fell into a deep sleep.

Chapter Five. Thebes...

"Adrienne, you will wake on a count of five. One, two, feeling relaxed and refreshed, three, four, almost there, five awake, feeling fine in every way."

Adrienne was looking up, seeing only white tiles at first.

"Adrienne, how do you feel?"

Slowly at first, Adrienne responded.

"Oh, fine, Dr. Hart."

She asked.

"How did the session go?"

Dr. Hart responded.

"Wonderful, really could not have been better."

"Adrienne, we have a focus on the timing. From everything we've heard, it sounds like the timeframe around the 18th to the 20th dynasties. The Empire, as some call it, was a high point of Egyptian history. We also have some sketches that you have made under hypnosis, showing the temple and its position in the ancient city of Thebes. We can now identify the religion and your position in it as 'The Chosen' high priestess of the personage considered to be your father, the sun god, Ra. We know many of the ruins still exist. We may be fortunate and pinpoint the temple and if those young skeletal remains can be found, or any other related proof of similar nature, your experience in a past life will be validated."

Adrienne spoke after a moment:

"Dr. Hart, I want to go on the search. The sketches are very good but I can help direct the search party. I can help you and I need to settle all of this for myself and for all the other people like me."

Dr. Hart pondered the question. As he looked at her intense facial expression, he finally said,

"Well, I don't think it would be any problem to arrange additional passage. Depending on the present condition of the ruins, you will be the most contributing member of our party in narrowing down the location sites. Your idea makes a great deal of sense, so you will join us in Egypt"

Dr. Hart continued,

"Adrienne, you rest here, I'm going down the hall. I will have my secretary contact the airlines, hotels, etc., there are so many things to do and we only have a couple of days. Is your passport current? We will need to check on our inoculations also. First things first. You wait here and I'll be back in about fifteen minutes."

As the door closed behind Dr. Hart, Adrienne looked at Hans. Even with all of this excitement she could not help but notice that Hans was really very handsome. She had somehow been naturally drawn to him when she met him. The more time she spent with him, the more comfortable she was with him. She felt as though she would like to get to know him better.

"Hans, how long have you been involved with doing validation work?"

Hans thought for a moment.

"Oh, for about five years. I started with a part-time project and then the work just seemed to take up more and more of my time. I began my first full-time project three years ago. Before that I was teaching full time working and traveling with validation teams in the summer months when I was not on campus."

Adrienne thought for a few moments and then said, "It is an unusual path for college professor to take. What prompted your interest?"

Hans stared out the window for very long time. He struggled with how to answer her question. Hans felt as though he could trust Adrienne. He decided to just be honest about his comments.

"Well Adrienne, I had so many experiences when I was a child and I seemed to be very drawn to spiritual concepts and values that came from another time in history. It is difficult to explain. I decided to attempt to explore these interests and try to find some clearer explanations for myself. I studied and traveled and began to meet people who had experienced similar situations. Validation work had been going on worldwide for many years. Major learning institutions were working on several highly publicized studies. The academic verification process seemed to be the only validation tool that would gain society's understanding and eventual acceptance."

Adrienne was surprised by the response.

"Hans, I had no idea that you have had some similar experiences to mine. I thought…"

Her voice paused for a moment. Hans commented,

"Did you feel you were the only one this could be happening to?"

"No, I guess not, but it is still a new experience for me to meet anyone who even marginally accepts my life occurrences as realities. Meeting with someone who really understands my experience is wonderful. It leaves me feeling a little less crazy."

"Is that you what you thought Adrienne, that you were crazy?"

"Well, in all honesty I always felt that the experiences were very real, but because I did not know anyone else who had these experiences, I could not help but wonder about what was going on with me."

"Adrienne, when you decided you would explore this experience personally and eventually professionally with others in this field, you then opened the door to meeting other people who had similar experiences to yours. You will be pleasantly surprised as you began to find out, as I have, how many others there are."

Dr. Hart walked into the room.

"The arrangements have begun. I think we should break for lunch."

Suddenly Adrienne realized how much of the day had gone by, and she was in fact very hungry.

"Lunch sound great, I am ready when you are."

As they walked down the corridor together she felt so much more secure in her feelings about the future. For the first time in quite a while, she had a sense that she was on the right path.

Chapter Six. The Journey Begins…

Egypt was incredible! Adrienne had never traveled such a great distance. This trip was emotionally charged for her because she was so close to finding out some tangible information about her past life in Egypt. She had been disappointed that she could not spend more time with her brother after his retreat. His arrival to spend a few days with her came about at the same time she and Dr. Hart had agreed on the trip. Her visit with her brother had been cut a little short. Adrienne did not want to burden him with the concerns she had about this journey. He was in the middle of making a very important decision regarding his life in the priesthood. They spent a lot of time talking about his feelings regarding how best to continue his spiritual life. It seemed to help him to talk about this conflict he was struggling with. They agreed that while they would have liked to spend a little more time together, he needed to take some time to go back to his parish. Mike needed to talk with his mentor and meditate on his future. Mike did not mind having a little less time with his sister, as he was aware that the plans to go to Egypt had been made with many

44

other people in mind. They agreed to spend more time together after her visit to Eqypt.

While Adrienne's personal schedule had been disrupted, the visit to Egypt was amazing. To read about such an incredible city was one thing, but to see these monumental sites was quite another. It was really hot and the sun was shining brightly. She soon found out that during the height of the sun remaining in the hotel was the best thing to do. As she looked out the window of her hotel, she began to study the city. The rooftops were all so different in color and the materials they were made of, that they provided quite a contrast to the eye. The walls of some of the buildings had been painted white. The sun shining upon them was blinding. The validation team would be leaving this city and flying by helicopter to Thebes tomorrow. She was nervous at the thought of such an important day. The knocking at her door drew her thoughts back from Thebes. Adrienne walked across the spacious marble tiled floors. A slight breeze pushed the gauze like curtains away from the huge windows.

"Who is it?"

"Adrienne, its Hans. Can I come in?"

Adrienne opened the door.

"Hans, how are you? I was wondering where you were today"

"Shopping in the market, madam. I am here to show you the fruits of my labor."

Hans pulled out a beautiful full-length turquoise colored silk gown. The style was very free flowing and loose. Small, silk, blue-green rosettes were fashioned as buttons.

Adrienne just stared at it, amazed at the colors and softness of the material.

"Hans it's beautiful!"

"Nothing less would do, Adrienne. As soon as I saw it, I knew I had to buy for you."

"It's perfect", Adrienne said, "I will wear this when we return from Thebes for our last night's celebration dinner."

Hans smiled.

"I hope that doesn't mean we have to wait for our last night in Thebes to have dinner together. I found an intriguing restaurant about a block from the hotel. It is definitely the kind of place everyone should visit once in their lives, if possible."

Adrienne smiled.

"Well, it sounds like something I should not miss then! What about dinner in two hours? It should be a lot cooler then and I'll have time to nap, shower and change clothes."

Hans replied, "Sounds good to me. I will meet you in the main lobby in two hours. Until then, I will say goodbye and be on my way."

Adrienne waved, watching as Hans left the room. As the door closed, her eyes slowly looked around the room. She was drawn again to the window to a view that was memorable.

Stark window shades reflecting sunshine in a myriad of conflicting patterns. Adrienne marveled at the consistently busy level of activity outside. Men, women, children and animals were moving like a river flowing, through the narrow streets and alleys. The colors diverse, dancing and the momentum never-ending. She pushed the wooden slats aside. Looking directly down, she watched a small child walking behind her mother. The child's footsteps were rapid in their pace to keep up with her mother's longer strides. As the two disappeared around the corner, Adrienne glanced at her watch. She realized if she were going to get any rest before dinner, she would have to pull herself away from the window.

She pulled the wooden slats closed. As she walked away from the window, the cool sensation of the marble floors felt very soothing. Adrienne sat down on the high bed and pulled the mosquito netting down around the sides of the bed. She lay down and looked out through the netting. Her hotel suite looked so muted through the gauze netting. She felt very comfortable and relaxed. Closing her eyes she drifted into a very restful sleep.

Chapter Seven. An Old Enemy Returns...

The heat. She felt so unbearably hot, so warm she had difficulty getting any air to breathe.

Dark, why so dark?

She felt frightened, threatened, something was wrong. Her mind was rising in panic, simultaneously feeling pressure. Such a heavy pressure. She tried to move and could not, her panic now increased. Something was pressing on her. Adrienne's eyes blinked open. The room was intensely hot. The physical fright of feeling that she was unable to draw the breath that she needed to survive was almost paralyzing to her. Then, for a moment, she was completely still, her body frozen. She was looking straight up at a sight that almost stopped her heart completely. The figure seemed two or even three times her size. It was hovering over her body. It took up all the oxygen in the room and the creature was emitting heat that was so intense, as though the room was about to burst into flames. The creature was so close. As it drew closer, the pressure and heat Adrienne had awoken to increased. The face was beyond imagination-demonic, and horrific. She felt physical and mental shock and it immobilized her completely. Her mind froze. She had never felt death so close.

The thought of the finality of her situation slowly stirred some part of her incredibly frightened spirit. She began to talk to herself:

Fight! It's your last chance, don't give in.

Adrienne tried to open her mouth, a desperate attempt to get some air.

A dream, this must be a dream, pull yourself away. Wake up, try to wake...now! Adrienne was mentally shouting. Dream or not she felt as though she was dying. She forced her eyes to open she used all her strength to lift her head from the pillow.

I will get up. This will all go away, if I just get up.

Adrienne could barely lift her head from the bed. She tried to move in any direction. She was pinned to the bed. She realized with fear beginning to shake her consciousness that she was not asleep. This was no dream. She had no sensation of any breath, no oxygen left at all. She was numbed, her senses completely in shock. She could see clearly but she was afraid to look again. She was determined to force herself to look and see if the apparition was really still there. She steeled herself and forced her eyes to look up again. The manifestation was beyond her wildest imagination. The pure essence of evil reeked from this creature. There was power in its glare, great power. Her mind was almost completely frozen with fear. That face. It looked liked an animal of some kind, but also like a man. The whole body had hair covering it, hornlike protrusions, and teeth that were huge and sharp. It was drooling on her through its teeth, and emitting a low growling sound. It was almost grinning, enjoying her fear. It was completely on top of her, its hands with their long nails running up her arms. Adrienne felt that she was on the brink of dying. A death that was so horrible and so incredible to her psyche, it was beyond her sense of reality. In fact, she realized this was beyond reality, beyond this dimension, and for a moment she felt hopeless. She was so close to losing consciousness. Somewhere in her mind, a voice whispered,

One chance. Focus:

As from a lesson learned long ago, her spirit stirred.

Focus and allow your spirit guides to provide you with protection.

Her mind began to envision a spiritual presence.

Her eyes closed. She joined her spirit with the guides that were here to help her and she prayed. This was all that was left, all that could save her, if she were to be spared. If that was her destiny, then so be it. She imagined the white cloak of the spiritual guides covering her, protecting her, and she merged that reality in her mind. Her will grew stronger, she could feel it. She felt her concentration clear a bit more. She kept her focus, she had to, in her desperate attempt to avoid this foul and cursed death.

Time passed. She was not aware of how much time. The pressure on her body seemed to be gone although the room still felt much warmer than normal. She still had her eyes shut, but decided to try to breathe. What an incredible relief as she drew a breath. Adrienne lay still. She was afraid to open her eyes. She realized she would have to push herself and fight the fear. Her eyes fluttered open. Adrienne's clear blue eyes glanced quickly, *Nothing but the furniture, the creature is gone, she thought.* She tried to get up. She was weak but too afraid to let herself sit and gain strength. She pushed her legs over the side of her bed and began to try to walk toward the door. She tripped and fell with weakness. She crawled forward and stood up again and went toward the door. She left the room, heading for the hall and finally the elevator.

When the doors opened on the street level, she was thrilled to see other people and somehow felt safer. She sat in the first large chair she came to. Adrienne had never had such an experience

What does this mean? Why me? Where is there safety from something like that?

She was very frightened. She wondered what kind of future she was heading for, if she survived at all. What kind of an existence would she have if monsters could invade her reality? When spiritual realms could merge and allow such a creature to almost take her life. She sat amid the hustle and bustle of the huge hotel in Egypt, the palm trees, the people, everything, now looked and seemed so mundane. Compared to what had just happened to her, she sensed something quite the opposite from mundane was about to unfold.

Adrienne sat in the lobby trying to get herself to a point of feeling more grounded, to diminish her fear. Suddenly, a voice startled her, Madam?"

She looked up into the face of a hotel employee. His crisp, starched white jacket bending stiffly as he politely asked if she would like a drink or a cup of tea. She stared blankly at him for a few moments and realized she had been in the lobby for quite some time.

"No, no thank you," she stammered.

"I must call my friend, can you direct me to the hotel lobby phone?"

He pointed her in the right direction and Adrienne felt herself rise up from the chair, slowly approaching the phone. She picked it up and asked the hotel operator to connect her call to Hans' room.

As soon as she heard his voice, she told Hans she needed his help and told him she was in the lobby. She barely heard his words as he said he would be right down. He instructed her to find a place to sit down. Before Adrienne knew it, Hans sat down beside her.

"Adrienne, what's wrong?"

"Hans, I'm scared. I've had the most frightening experience in my life."

"Adrienne, can you walk?"

She responded, "Yes, I think so."

Hans said, "Let's go up to my room. I'll call Dr. Hart to join us."

Adrienne nodded. She walked with Hans to the elevator. She felt numb, oblivious to all of the activity surrounding her. She felt his hand firmly holding her arm. Hans unlocked the door, walked Adrienne across the room, and helped her sit down. He called Dr. Hart, explaining briefly that Adrienne had suffered some kind of shock and asked him to come up to his room.

Hans hung up the telephone, went to the small refrigerator and opened the door.

Slowly reviewing the complimentary bottles inside, he pulled out the small bottle of Jamison's Irish whiskey and a small bottle of Perrier water, "Adrienne, sip this. It will help relax you."

Adrienne automatically took the glass without question, drank some and sat back. Dr. Hart arrived, his face full of concern. He asked that she be propped up on the bed. He pulled a coverlet up almost to her chin. Dr. Hart asked Hans to call room service for soup, soda crackers, herbal tea and a double brandy.

Dr. Hart pulled a chair close to the bed.

"Adrienne, I've called for some food. Tell me, what has happened to you?"

"Doctor, it was so unreal. I know I didn't imagine it, or dream it, but it defies my reality. That is the really frightening thing."

"Adrienne, tell me, what defies reality? What exactly happened?"

"I've seen the most horrifying manifestation of evil."

Adrienne's speech was slow, searching.

"Some kind of demon, or devil. I don't know. I really felt that I came so close to death itself. The paralyzing fear, and the intense heat and suffocating pressure. I am truly amazed that I survived. What's happening, Dr. Hart?"

Dr. Hart took her hand, his voice was soft and low.

"Adrienne, you are gifted. You and I have discovered natural inclinations that you were born with. Traits you had worked to suppress because you were afraid of your differences. Your psyche is of an ancient origin. Your origins are so complex that much more information will need to be obtained before we can understand this phenomenon. We do know, from the tapes we've recorded so far, that you have some very old spiritual ties. It would seem that from your past life experiences there are many strong forces in conflict. Conflict between the dark and light has existed since the beginning of time. You are, it would seem, somehow in serious conflict with the dark sides of these forces."

A sharp knock at the door startled Adrienne.

"Room service."

Hans opened the door and the waiter rolled in a large tray covered with silver and crystal. Hans tipped the waiter and told him he would serve the food himself. As the door closed the scent of spices and food drifted throughout the room. Hans pulled the tray alongside the bed. Dr. Hart spoke first, "Adrienne, I would like to call my colleagues back in the States to help us do some additional research on this experience you have had. Hans will help you with dinner. I will leave two tablets for you to take after your dinner to help you sleep. Hans, I think you should stay here for the night. I will call the hotel for a cot. Call me if you need me for any reason. I've got some maps and manuscripts to review before tomorrow's visit to Thebes. We will need the additional information to find the temple we are seeking. The validation is critical to this trip. I've arranged for two representatives from the University of Cairo and an affiliated museum to be with us. One of their staff photographers will assist us with photos."

Hans and Adrienne watched the doctor leave. Hans picked up the silver dome. The soup was hearty looking. The tureen was huge; there was enough soup for four. As they shared some dinner, Adrienne felt more like herself and a little more relaxed. After the cot arrived, they shared some brandy. The view of the city was really spectacular. They finally decided to turn in for the night. Although Adrienne had insisted Hans leave the lights on so she would not be in the dark, she could still see the lights outside. They were beautiful, reminding her of all the good things in the world. Eventually she took the two tablets and fell asleep while looking at the skyline of Egypt.

The telephone rang loudly and with a shrill echo. Adrienne woke up, startled. She grabbed the telephone receiver, managing a weak greeting.

"Hello?"

"Adrienne? It's Dr. Hart, how are you feeling?"

"I'm fine. Much better today, thank you."

"I am so glad to hear that"

"Adrienne, I've arranged for breakfast in an hour. Is that sufficient time for you to freshen up?"

"Oh, yes. I will meet you in the lobby at 9:30. See you then."

Adrienne woke Hans.

"We are supposed to meet Dr. Hart at 9:30 for breakfast."

Hans lifted his head and said sleepily,

"Okay. I'll be down to meet you in thirty minutes."

Adrienne put on her shoes, saying,

"I'll go to my room and get ready. See you in a half-hour."

She stopped by the door.

"Hans, thank you so much for staying with me."

Hans smiled and waved her a sleepy goodbye.

Adrienne was ready in no time. Closing the door behind her, she walked quickly toward the elevator. She pushed the button and waited. She stared down at the plush red carpet. The gold design flowed boldly along the border. She realized that she really enjoyed the thought of Hans meeting her and having breakfast together. She had never felt this way about any man she had known before. The thought surprised her. The elevator door opened, she glanced at her watch and realized she had to hurry.

Adrienne, Hans and Dr. Hart scanned their menus. The dishes ranged from bland to the exotic.

Everyone decided without really discussing it that the blander foods would be the best choice for such a busy day. Adrienne enjoyed the scents coming from the kitchen; the curry, peppers and spices created an enticing combination. She looked around the room. The crisp linen tablecloths and the heavy silverware, everything seemed so regulated, so predictable. It was so difficult to believe that her frightening experience of last night had been real. Dr. Hart interrupted her train of thought.

"Adrienne, are you really up to going on the tour?"

Her eyes, so deep blue, were fixed on his face. So many confusing emotions ran behind that steady gaze.

"Dr. Hart, I must be up to it. My mental piece of mind hinges on clarifying this mystery. I want to stop being an enigma. I need to understand what exactly is happening and why. You have helped me to understand so much. Now I need to complete the puzzle."

"If you are that sure, we will push ahead. I must make a call to arrange for a cab. While some of the others are flying we are taking the train and bringing some of the heavier equipment with us. The train departs for Thebes in one hour. Let's meet in the lobby in thirty minutes. The cab will be waiting."

Dr. Hart pushed away his empty plate and coffee cup. He handed an envelope to Adrienne and Hans.

"In case we get separated at the station, here are your tickets."

He pushed his chair away from the table.

"See you in a half-hour."

Adrienne realized the time was getting short and said "I am going to head back to my room. I want to finish packing my suitcase, so I will meet you in front of the hotel when the cab arrives.

Hans replied,

"Okay, I'll see you then. I'm going to have a quick second cup of coffee."

As Adrienne walked away, Hans watched her as she left the room. He felt she was very special and he felt very protective of her in some way. It really surprised him as he was accustomed to treating everyone equally. He felt so different about Adrienne. He couldn't help but feel that she could be the kind of person he could share his life with. He also realized that with so much happening in their lives at this time, he should not be thinking about a romantic commitment. His personal feelings and his years of validation studies seemed to be culminating at last. Thebes would hold a lot of answers.

Chapter Eight. Evil Personified…

The cab pulled up to an incredibly confusing scene. People of all sizes and colors rushed quickly around. The heat, the scents and sounds of animals filled the air. All three travelers rushed through the crowds toward the train platform for Thebes. A beggar pushed in front of Dr. Hart. A stream of goats followed, flowing in three different directions. Adrienne was half-way to the platform when she realized she was alone. She stopped and looked around. There were no familiar faces. The loudspeaker cracked and announced information in some unknown language. Steam hissed loudly from under the train.

"Adrienne."

She turned to the sound of the voice and saw Hans at the steps of the train. He was waving her on. She ran toward the train. They rushed up the small steps of the train, and began looking for their compartments.

"Did you see Dr. Hart?"

"No, but the agreement was, even if we were separated, that we should get on the train and we would meet at our destination."

As they walked toward their compartments, they decided after they got settled they would go to the club car for a chilled drink. Finding the compartments, they threw their luggage inside and headed for the lounge. They slid into the large, comfortable chairs. Ordering two cold drinks, they sat back in the chairs. They quietly looked out at the desert-like countryside. Hans pulled the window shade half way down to shelter them from the rays of the sun. When the drinks arrived, they sipped them and began to cool down and relax. Adrienne watched Hans, his hair and eyes reflecting the light of the sunshine. She was definitely attracted to him. He was thoughtful, sensitive and intelligent, and really had very handsome features. She was so accustomed to being alone and independent. She wondered if she could really feel comfortable with a serious long-term commitment. She knew that it would have to be with a very special person.

So far no one had impressed her enough to commit herself to. Hans was the first person she had really considered having a serious relationship with, but it was such a big decision, she decided to put it all out of her mind for now.

"Hans, do you mind waiting for a moment? I am going to find the restroom and freshen up."

"I'd wait for you forever, madam," he commented, with a grand sweep of the hand. She laughed and walked down the corridor. The cool water felt wonderful as she splashed her arms and face. Somehow, knowing she would soon be in Thebes made her feel more confident that she was close to more evidence of her past life. She was feeling so much better about that progress. She felt a little more in control about everything.

As she learned more about her past, her future was becoming clearer. She put some light lip gloss on and a light brush of blush on her cheeks and pulled her hair back with two mother-of- pearl combs. She put everything back in her purse, pulled open the door and began to walk along the narrow corridor. The train gently rocked as she walked straight ahead. She looked up and saw a man walking toward her. As he drew closer, she slowed down, realizing it would be a tight squeeze. As they began to pass each other, the man suddenly turned toward her pushing her up against the wall. His eyes were paralyzing to look at. They seemed yellow and were oddly shaped. His strength was overpowering. He hissed as he spoke,

"You are very beautiful in spirit and in flesh. You would be a supreme sacrifice. If you come to Thebes you will challenge me. I would enjoy your struggle."

His face was so close. He ran one finger with a long, sharp nail down from the middle of her throat to the cleft between her breasts. A thin stream of blood appeared.

"Perhaps you would enjoy the conflict also, Shanta?" His voice hissed.

The heat and lack of breath from being pressed so hard against the wall began to take effect. Adrienne began to feel faint. Things around her darkened into total blackness.

"Adrienne, Adrienne."

She heard her name. She felt so confused. She opened her eyes and saw Hans looking troubled. He was pressing a cold cloth on her forehead, face and arms.

"Adrienne, we shouldn't have come so soon. Perhaps we should have stayed at the hotel for a few more days. You must be more exhausted than we thought."

"The man. Where is the man?"

"Man? What are you talking about?"

"This strange man, he accosted me, pushed me against the wall."

Hans stared at her, asking incredulously,

"Someone assaulted you?"

Hans looked up and down the hall, seeing no one. He shook his head, with concern asking himself

What next?

Hans asked Adrienne,

"Can you walk?"

Adrienne felt so confused. Still trying to feel joined to the rest of her limbs, she felt somewhat numb.

"Hans, I'll lean on you. Let's get out of the corridor."

Hans and Adrienne slowly walked to her compartment. Hans opened the silver-handled door knob. Adrienne sat down on the plush, comfortable cushions. She was so confused.

Who was that man? He seemed to know me, knew my name. He seemed to be someone who celebrated violence, talking about welcoming conflict with me.

A sharp knock at the door startled her. Hans went to open the door. Adrienne gestured for him to stop. Hans stopped and called out.

"Who is it?"

A familiar voice said,

"It's me,

"Dr. Hart?"

Hans recognized his voice and opened the door. Dr. Hart walked in, and asked,

"What are you both looking so troubled about?"

They both began to explain at once. Dr. Hart listened very carefully. He leaned forward and clasped Adrienne's hands.

"Adrienne, when you had what I would call a psychic assault at the hotel, I knew we were up against a difficult adversary. I have worked with people in many countries for over twenty years. I have learned a lot from them, and they continue to help me. When you were threatened physically from another dimension at the hotel, I sent data, including some tape recordings of our sessions, to some of my colleagues. Some of them are experts in the ancient religions. I do not have all of their feedback yet. However, what I do have is startling. The group that you were chosen to be the leader of was a very old, very powerful group. This group was very protective of their beliefs and the members of their group. They would make sure to be represented in the mainstream religious and political circles. They were highly visible, intelligent, influential and frequently of great prestige. They use their positions to assist in their main goal to protect their inner circle. We have collected some information showing that they were pervasive in ancient society and subversive when necessary. Their training and commitment to the group was for life. It began at birth. From that point on everything was done for the survival and propagation of the group. Women seemed to have great power in this group. From early periods of their history, we can find that women often ruled the group. One woman, based on special psychic capabilities, which were deemed present at birth and developed with training, was called *the chosen*. It was said this woman would have immense power according to a quote from one of their writings, "Spanning all time, all dimensions, to hold and enhance the influence of the entire order".

The few ancient records we have seen suggest information that we cannot match up yet, information about a circle of people and a continuum that we don't understand yet. I have written to several other colleagues for some information that still hasn't been sent back to me. But Adrienne, know this: Your adversary is an old one, and a strong one. In addition, this influence has made it clear to you that you are threatening to it. This man, or whatever he was, when he appeared to you, mentioned Thebes. So, if he knows our destination, something else awaits us there besides my two colleagues assisting in the validation."

"Dr. Hart," Adrienne hesitated, "I'm afraid, but I can't turn back. I don't know why, and it seems ridiculous under the circumstances, but I'm feeling as though we must move ahead."

All three sat close together, quietly pondering the future of this dangerous venture. The ominous nature of the project was definitely intimidating.

"Tickets! Tickets!"

Hans rose from his chair, he pulled his wallet from his pocket, drew the ticket voucher out, and opened the door. The ticket collector looked at the information, punched the ticket and returned it to Hans. Adrienne and Dr. Hart completed the same process. The door shut and after a few minutes of thoughtful silence, Dr. Hart brought up the idea of a change of scene. He suggested going to the dining room car for some food and then to bed. Their stop at Thebes would be early in the morning. It would make sense to get good nights sleep.

Chapter Nine. The Bones Tell a Tale…

Thebes, what a sight.

Adrienne stood on a hill, seeing white stucco buildings of all shapes and sizes. She felt as though she had a familiarity of sorts, but the impression was recalling buildings of larger dimensions, different shapes. Then she remembered, those were different times. Her thoughts were interrupted as it was time to resume the trip to the site.

Camels ready, supplies loaded, they began their ride. The temples were visible in the distance, but still perhaps another half-hour ride. Her view of the temple site was clear, but her mind was troubled, as the man's threats on the train still frightened her. Would he show up here, or somewhere else, the uncertainly was very unsettling. The camels' strides were swift. They rapidly approached the old temple site. At first, in the distance, the ruins all looked the same. They were in a state of complete disrepair, portions of the stones in fallen heaps. The wind blew through the remaining stones, which were worn down from years of being exposed to the harsh elements of the desert. Adrienne could see more detail as they approached the site, outlines of the foundations of the building stills remained, and she could almost imagine the city as it had once been.

The camels were herded toward makeshift stables. As Adrienne dismounted, she could see a small group of people approaching the stable. The camels came to a standstill, kneeling to allow everyone to slide down from the high saddles. Dr. Hart greeted the team that was waiting. Hans recognized all of the people, he had met them on past projects, and he smiled as he walked toward them. They all shook hands and Dr. Hart walked the group toward the shaded stable where Adrienne was standing and said.

"Adrienne, let me introduce Dr. Ona Inkda, Mr. Gene Shendal, Ms. Gina Dindae. These are colleagues who specialize in historical validation process work."

These people are the best in the field. Ona has written several books on validated cases."

Ona interjected,

"Many thanks for your praise. I am looking forward to working with you again, especially on this case."

She turned her eyes toward Adrienne, saying,

"This case is close to my interests because of a trace of my own background that I am working on. But those facts can be reviewed later. The heat is increasing, and the daylight hours are half gone, shall we begin?"

Everyone agreed. They all began to pick up their equipment, video, voice recorders, lights, everything needed to document this occasion.

As they walked, Dr. Inkda commented,

"The oldest temples are on the inside circle of ruins. They were built first. As the decades passed and the communities increased in size, additional buildings were added ultimately spreading the circle outward. We will start with the interior circle because, from the tapes Dr. Hart sent, your religious origin is of the most ancient order."

Adrienne looked at the doctor asking,

"You know something about the order?"

Ona looked into Adrienne's clear blue-green eyes, saying,

"Yes, but this is not the time for us to talk of this matter. We can talk more freely after today's filming."

The group slowly approached the central buildings. Adrienne stopped and turned around. The group followed her steps. She looked up, squinting at the bright sun. The rays felt so strong.

Adrienne somehow recalled, however distantly, a ceremony. *The sun.* Yes, the position of the sun and the memory of her self standing with her arms raised. She turned, and her arms began to rise. She heard the click and whirring of something, an annoying sound, which distracted her thoughts. She turned her head toward the noise and saw the video equipment. The filming then stopped, as it was clear it had broken the flow of her concentration.

"Ona, this month!"

"Yes, the time of Ra."

"The way the sun sits."

Adrienne's voice trailed away. The group stopped talking and moving around and stared at her.

Adrienne looked back out across the horizon.

"Dr. Hart, I know now. That building, the one with the plateau jutting toward the sun that is our destination."

She began to walk. They all followed Adrienne's quick pace. She walked with some dim recollection of the area. As she entered the ruins and continued walking. The remaining walls were cracked and peeling, the wall paintings chipped and faded by time and the elements. Somehow, she knew the path of the corridors well.

Four doorways from here.

She stopped and looked into what once was a room. She crossed this area to the portals. Adrienne stared at the floor for a few minutes. Ona asked that the video and taping begin. Adrienne remembered the lesson. She knelt down and felt the floor. The crack was there. She pushed the stone away. They watched as an opening appeared. Adrienne called to Dr. Hart,

"This is the place. The tunnel runs under the room. The passage is very small, enough room for a person to walk in slouched position."

Dr. Hart called to Gina.

"Gina, you are the smallest. Will you take the camera and drop down to see if there are any visible skeletal remains? If you see anything at all, film it."

Gina nodded. Pulling the small camera close, she inched into the small tunnel. She turned on the camera; the light flooded the area. The dust of the ages clung to the walls. The earth below her feet felt very loose and sandy. She slowly walked in somewhat of a slouched fashion. Filming everything as she walked, the light from the camera illuminated the area and made her feel better about being in such a small space. She continued down the tunnel. It was cumbersome to walk in such an awkward position and trying to support the camera made it more difficult. Gina felt so alone, and very nervous. She wished she could be outside again. This tunnel was hot, dusty, dark, and the walls were so close together. She felt isolated in this seemingly endless tunnel, separated completely from the group.

Her foot bumped into something. She backed up and kept filming. She turned the camera down toward the floor of the tunnel. She was stunned to see a small skull. It must have been hidden by the deep sand and dust. She knelt gently down and looked very closely. She saw a rib cage and leg bones; they were the remains of a human body, a petite body. A small piece of metal reflected through the dust. A gold chain with some kind of charm was attached. Gina gently picked up what appeared to be a necklace and put it in a plastic bag. She then took a small sample of the dirt, and one section of bone, keeping them in separate plastic bags and putting them in her pocket. This was amazing, just as Dr. Hart and Adrienne had transcribed from the regression tapes. Adrienne's body from when she lived as Shanta in Egypt, so long ago.

Gina shouted out to let the others know she was coming back. She slowly inched her way back. As the camera equipment was passed up through the passage everyone clustered around Gina. The tension and excitement became even greater than the excessive heat of the day. Dr. Hart, Gene, Hans, Adrienne and Ona all seemed to ask at once,

"Did you see anything?"

Gina crawled through the space.

"Adrienne, it was all just as you said. The bones and a necklace were there. I have brought back some samples for you and Dr. Hart I filmed everything on the video camera."

Cheers resounded in the corridors. Adrienne, was stunned, the reality of Gina's comments resounded in her mind. This discovery was a shock to Adrienne. Her life as Shanta had suddenly become very concrete to her as she looked at the sample bags Gina had brought back. Bags containing the bones that had once belonged to her body from another time, and a personal piece of jewelry that she had worn in that same period. Adrienne's life changed at that moment, any doubt that she had about pursuing the truth in her life disappeared. She was infused with such hope for the future, knowing that even more clarity on her past life as Shanta would be forthcoming. Life was full of miracles, and she had just witnessed one of them.

Chapter Ten. The Necklace and

The Circle...

Once back at the hotel, Dr. Hart and Dr. Inkda made arrangements with the Egyptian university to have a team of archeologists work on the newly discovered remains. Gene and Gina would stay in Egypt and head up the team based there. Once that was all arranged, everyone agreed to freshen up and meet for dinner in the air-conditioned dining area; it would be a well-earned respite and celebration. Some of the team members begged off from dinner. They were so excited they decided to go to the university to meet with the new team and look over the new artifacts and films.

As everyone relaxed with chilled drinks, Dr. Hart began the discussion.

"We have formally validated some of Adrienne's past life. The archeologists will work on the process for excavating and dating the skeletal remains we discovered."

Gina handed an envelope to Dr. Hart. The necklace was inside.

"This was in the tunnel, beside the skeleton. Dr. Hart."

He looked inside the envelope.

"Gina, it's beautiful; priceless."

Dr. Hart turned the charm around. It was a circle with protrusions of gold.

It appeared to be made to look like the sun. He turned it around in his hand.

"There's an inscription on the back."

Ona looked it over.

"Let me see the writing perhaps I can read it. I have studied the old languages for years."

Ona brushed away some dust. She studied the etchings closely, pulled out a magnifying glass and looked again.

"It says, Ra protects and the circle comes together."

"Ona, what does it mean?"

"Well, of what we know thus far, Adrienne's past life as Shanta had her represented as 'the Chosen One" The group appears to be comprised of high priests and priestesses in service to the sun god, Ra. Ra was thought to be creator and high god of the universe. So, Ra protects. The circle must have referred to the spiritual group. But to 'come together'? In this old language, 'rejoin', I'm not sure of the entire context of the phrase. Adrienne might be able to help us if we asked her more about this in one of her regression sessions. We can get specific information that will be valued as definitive now that we have such credible validation for the general public."

Dr. Hart pondered her comments and finally said,

"We will have to stop for today. Tonight, let's plan to celebrate the culmination of everyone's labor."

Adrienne sat with Hans and wore the beautiful dress he had bought for her in the marketplace.

The dinner that evening was festive, with various foods that were exotically spicy. The group members were cheerful and everyone was having a wonderful time. The group decided to adjourn early for bed, having all had an exciting, yet tiring day. Before they left the team toasted each other, Dr. Hart and Adrienne for all they had accomplished. Before everyone retired for the evening, a meeting was scheduled for the following day at Ona's offices at the university.

Adrienne awoke early in the morning. The sights from her hotel window were so intriguing. She thought,

I must go see the shops.

She had so much energy and she had to wait hours before the meeting. She decided to go for a walk. With great haste she set off for the markets. She walked the streets looking at the colorful carts. Birds fluttered in straw makeshift cages. People in many different colored outfits, hats and various shaped shoes wandered in every direction. The browsing relaxed her. The days had been so intense lately. Fear and anxiety were a challenging combination of emotions for anyone. Adrienne's eyes slowly glanced at the carts and stands that people's wares were shown for sale upon. She stopped, seeing some stone etchings. She walked up to the stand and touched one of the stones. Leaning closer, she observed the intricacy of the sketches. She imagined the many hours that someone must have worked on the piece. It was lovely; perhaps this would make a good memento for her trip. Suddenly she felt a grip on her arm. It was painful and as cold as ice. Adrienne gasped at the shock. She turned her head and looked directly into what appeared to be a human face, but the eyes looked like those of a cat, yellow pupils slanted, piercing. The grasp on her arm was still tight.

"Shanta, you pursue such a dangerous path. Pursue no further or you will die."

The voice thundered in her ears. She felt as though her eardrums would shatter.

Adrienne broke free and ran. She kept running, never looking back. Fright motivated her speed. She saw the hotel and ran into the lobby. Feeling safer in the crowded room, she sat down. She wondered what the man, or whatever it was, wanted. He seemed to be aware of every move she made, but why? Suddenly she realized he had called her "Shanta". She thought back to the train incident. Fright had suppressed her thoughts before, but now she remembered. He had used the name "Shanta" on the train as well. She needed to know more about the mystery of Shanta's relationship to that thing. Why was it so intent on threatening her? Adrienne decided that as soon as her heart stopped pounding, she would leave a message for Dr. Hart to tell him what had happened to her.

Dr. Hart had finished the meeting at the university. The discussions were all filled with excitement, as all of the experts involved had been having such good progress with tests on the bones and other samples brought back from the Egyptian ruins.

The group decided they needed to document their work and prepare a report on what had occurred. They also concurred on the confirmation of arrangements to return to the United States. Also, that Adrienne would have to do some regression work to see if more information could be discovered.

Adrienne was thinking she would so feel relieved when she was back home. She would be safe at home. Adrienne wanted to believe everything would be just as it used to be. She wanted to believe that the dream and the stranger attacking her occurred because she was in Egypt. She had told her story of the occurrence in the marketplace to Dr. Hart, and while he understood her fear, he still did not have all of the answers as to why this thing focused only on her. But he assured Adrienne when they got home he would follow up and call some of his colleagues and see if they could help shed some light on Adrienne's dangerous predicament.

Chapter Eleven. Return From Egypt...

On the trip home she slept. It was pleasant to be on such a smooth flight, the temperature was so much cooler. The heat of Egypt was something Adrienne would not miss at all. She enjoyed the taste of American food served on the plane. She found the familiarity comforting. She felt a need for familiar things, her old routine, and her home. The recent string of new events was unsettling. She was so clearly aware of the need to clarify her questions. Who was she really? Obviously her feelings of being so different all those years were justified. Of course, that concern is what brought her to Dr. Hart initially. She was aware on some level of the importance of resolving all of her questions. There was a future purpose. Soon she would finally have the answers. Adrienne glanced out the window. She could see the airport getting closer; she was so happy to be home.

Adrienne looked forward to meeting Hans for dinner. A sharp knock sounded at the door. Adrienne walked quickly to the door.

When she opened it, she saw Hans holding a huge bouquet of fresh flowers.

"Hans, thank you. They are lovely! Please come in."

Adrienne thought he looked so handsome. He was so tanned from the trip, he looked even better than usual. Adrienne said,

"Would you like a glass of wine or something?"

"I'll have a mineral water if you're having something."

"Okay, let me put these flowers in water. Please, sit down. I'll be right back."

Hans sat in front of the window and looked out at the ocean. The sunset reflected on the water. It looked like a thousand diamonds. The view was great. He had always enjoyed watching the ocean. He realized how little time he had to be able to just sit and admire the water. The travel over the past few months had been excessive. This would be the last series of long trips he would make. A more settled existence really appealed to him, and now that the studies were winding down, he would settle and begin doing some serious writing about his research very soon.

"Hans, what are you thinking about?"

Adrienne handed him a chilled mineral water and she sipped a wine spritzer.

"Oh, just that I feel as if I've traveled the seven seas. I'm really looking forward to a more subdued lifestyle."

Adrienne looked out at the sunset; it really was a sight she never tired of seeing.

"Why have you had to go to so many places?" she asked.

"I've been collecting personal interviews and tapes of events relating to past life regression. I did not want the sources for my research to be hearsay. I wanted total accuracy and I felt I needed to validate the work first hand. My research has really dominated several months of my life. I stopped my work with Dr. Hart on my own personal past life validation to pursue the completion of my research work. I'll finish my personal exploration with him this year though. The time is near; I can feel it."

"Time is near? What do you mean?"

"Well, it's just an impression I have. I get what I call 'impressions' from time to time. I usually follow them. In the past they have always proven to be accurate."

"What do you mean? Do you think you are psychic?"

"I don't call it that. I've really just started paying attention to the tendency since I met Dr. Hart. I'm still getting used to learning to clarify the sensations, so I don't call the tendency anything except "impressions.""

Hans slowly put down his glass, asking,

"Shall we go to dinner?"

Adrienne sensed Hans wanted to change the subject.

"Sounds great! Let me get my sweater."

Adrienne picked up her sweater and pocketbook.

"Let's go."

"Your car or mine?"

she asked as they left the building; they were en route to what would prove to be a wonderful evening.

Adrienne slowly awakened. She squinted her eyes.

The sun seemed to come up early today,

she thought as she slowly glanced at her clock. Much to her surprise, it was later than she thought. She had to meet Dr. Hart for a session at 9:30. She made herself sit up. Mornings were always difficult for Adrienne, though, once she got going, she was fine.

She slowly walked toward the kitchen and began by putting on the coffee. While the coffee was brewing, she put the few dirty dishes into the dishwasher and turned it on. She opened the refrigerator and took out the orange juice and cream for the coffee.

She sipped her orange juice as she poured a mug of coffee. Adding the cream, she fumbled for a spoon. After drinking the glass of orange juice, she picked up her coffee mug and walked back towards the bathroom to take a shower. After showering and dressing, she was in the car on the way to Dr. Hart's office, feeling ready for another day.

As she pulled up to the university campus, she realized she was feeling really good. Her dinner date with Hans last evening was so special. She really enjoyed his company. In addition, she felt so enthusiastic about her progress with Dr. Hart. Her life made so much more sense to her now that she was working with the doctor. As she walked down the shiny linoleum-lined corridors she saw Dr. Hart coming from the other direction. He waved and smiled.

"Adrienne, how are you? Ready for our next session?"

They walked into the laboratory together.

"Yes, I'm really looking forward to continuing, doctor, now that we have proven my past Egyptian life. Going through that experience has helped me to pursue this work with more conviction."

The procedures of the hypnosis were so easy for Adrienne now. She began to relax as Dr. Hart turned on the recorder. A voice and video recording provided accurate records of all the occurrences.

Chapter Twelve. Secret Society...

Shanta stood in room as large as a cavern. Once again, she was at the tip of the pyramid but inside instead of out on the platform. She was the first in a processional line. The people formed a shape like a pyramid and, as they chanted, they changed their formation into a perfect circle. All joined hands; everyone was dressed in plain, white linen garb. Her mother's voice rang out,

"The bonding is complete. As it was in the beginning, is now and ever shall be. We keep the circle and the promise. Shanta will carry the circle to the appointed place and time. We will now join our thoughts."

Then there was silence. All hands held fast, all heads turned up. Mother had explained to Shanta that worship was a time for all powers to join and grow through and from each other. Shanta followed her training, relaxing herself, focusing on the circle and letting the flow of positive energy regenerate her being. When the joining was ended, she felt as if she were glowing. Everyone bowed once and left quietly through different exits. Shanta and her mother were together as they walked into one of the tunnels the group had used in the past. As they walked they passed the statue that seemed unisexual in nature, representing the masculine and feminine energies joined as one. Shanta asked her mother why the statue seemed to represent both male and female.

"Our 'circle' is to be sustained by both male and female in the order, with no distinction for differences of sex. The statue is combined in one to show this concept.

"Why do we meet here, mother?"

"Shanta, our spiritual practice must be protected. We have a destiny that cannot be interrupted. We keep the foundation of our beliefs hidden in the guise of other religions as required by the times we live in. The actual essence of our circle is protected by our silence to the death. Santa, we must be quiet now, this section of the tunnel is very close to the palace walls."

They walked along in silence.

Dr. Hart was softly calling Adrienne back to the present time. For the second time today, the sun beamed into Adrienne's eyes as she started to open them.

"Adrienne."

She nodded.

"Adrienne, would you like something to drink?"

"Yes, thanks."

He walked across the room, pulled the shade down a little, and opened the lab refrigerator door. He opened a soda container and poured some into a paper cup. As Adrienne sipped her drink she asked Dr. Hart how it went.

"I felt it was very helpful. It provides more information about your life and gave us more specifics about the spiritual order."

"What kind of information, Dr. Hart?"

"Well, Adrienne, you and your mother had a discussion about a very secret society. Apparently, the group you belonged to in Egypt was based on a highly regarded spiritual sect and within that sect, among some of its most highly esteemed members existed, a core or group of people who were protectors and participants of a very ancient spiritual practice."

Adrienne walked across the room and looked out the window. She was quiet for a moment. She turned and said,

"Dr. Hart, was there more? I must know everything."

"Adrienne, if it will help you, let's replay the tapes together."

"Can we do it now?" she asked eagerly.

"Well, Gina is scheduled to meet with me in a few minutes. You remember her from the dig? Gina was with Dr. Inkda. You remember the validation people?"

"Yes, she was the woman who found the piece of jewelry in the temple."

"One and the same. She is coming today with the results of the research the team in Egypt has found so far."

"Doctor, perhaps we could all talk together and compare information at the same time. What do you think?"

He thought for a moment and said,

"Why not? Do you feel up to it, Adrienne?"

"Yes, I would really welcome it. I'd like to get as much information as quickly as I can. I started all this to help me answer some questions about my feelings, the dreams, and so many other things. I feel a need to have a greater understanding about my dreams and my visions. There is no doubt that I'm tired, but my personal quest presses me on."

"Well, I'm to meet Gina in my office soon, so why don't you wait around, perhaps have some refreshment, and I will meet you at my office in, say, thirty minutes."

"See you then," Adrienne said and waved as she walked away. It felt good to be alone for a while. She enjoyed the walk along the old corridor. She always felt a sense of security from the well-polished sameness of the linoleum; probably from some past school memory. Always somewhat of a loner, she had spent years walking alone, looking down as she walked, reflecting on life. Many people enjoyed her company and she liked them as well, but there was always that feeling of otherness and needing more personal time alone to stay very clear and comfortable with the understanding of her distinct separateness.

She looked up and found herself at the door of the cafeteria. Sun was shining through the multi-pane door at the far end of the room. It was a welcome sight, and as the aroma of minestrone soup and coffee and meatloaf mingled, Adrienne was suddenly aware of how hungry she was. She also realized she had only about twenty minutes left a definite soup-and-sandwich time frame. She would have ten minutes to eat and ten minutes to walk back. She finished her lunch quickly, deciding that taking a different route back would be a nice change.

She walked through the cafeteria door into the college garden path. As she walked past a couple of small anthills, as was her usual habit, she carefully stepped around them, making sure not to step on them or on their home. She pondered what a wonderful thing it would be when all the regression work was done, to really be able to understand more about the origins of so many of her habits and the beliefs behind them, at long last.

"Adrienne, welcome. Please sit down. You remember Gina, don't you?"

"Yes, well it certainly is nice to see you again – and under air- conditioned circumstances."

They all laughed, remembering how stifling it was during their visit to Egypt.

"Well, Adrienne, it might have been hot, but our findings were well worth it."

Gina pulled up a file and continued.

"The necklace we took from the skeleton was very old, much older than the cloth remnants and the bones we also collected in Egypt. In fact, we analyzed the metal; it was a combination that we did not have recorded in the computer banks. It is a very high quality of gold and traces of an unknown metal, with a notation in a lost dialect stating that the sun oversees or watches. The phrase seems to say something like,

"We the circle, continue to come together, or come round full circle."

The interesting thing about the design of the necklace is that inside the gold circle is a platinum circle with a unisexual being etched in the center with nine small dots placed around the border of the circle."

They all sat in silence for a moment, and then Dr. Hart spoke.

"Gina, I thought we would combine our time together today, and it will certainly be of great interest to you to listen to the tapes of our most recent regression. So let's begin."

When they were all seated, Dr. Hart began to replay the recordings from Adrienne's recent hypnosis sequence. Everyone sat in silence as the new information was revealed.

Simultaneously, as the tape finished, they realized the direct correlation of information.

Dr. Hart looked at Gina and she said,

"The mention of the circle of nine – the tenth person at the center – and that Shanta will carry the circle, to the appointed place is very important information."

Dr. Hart interrupted,

"The unisexual being is mentioned as well."

"But, we still don't understand enough about this 'hidden or underlying spiritual group' that was mentioned. Perhaps that's why the necklace we found is so much older. We need to discover the reason why the order found it necessary to hide themselves within the guise of a more accepted religion. Why did they feel so threatened?"

Dr. Hart spoke first,

"Gina, can you extend your visit? Because, if you can remain with us, and Adrienne and I continue with our regression, we will use our combined academic and computer resources and expand our information base to resolve this mystery we have uncovered."

Gina began to review her schedule planner. She looked up and announced that her next seminar wasn't to be presented for two weeks. Gina decided to go to the library at Dr. Hart's location to see if there might be new information available on the ancient inscriptions she had discovered on the necklace. They all agreed to meet the next day and review all results of their work.

Chapter Thirteen. Teufelgeist-Demon

Ghost...

Adrienne decided to go to the supermarket and pick up something for dinner. As she walked across the parking lot toward the store, she noticed a street person huddled in a corner of the lot surrounded by bags. The person looked as though he had surrounded himself with trash, much like a makeshift barricade. Adrienne thought about the fact that there seemed to be so many more people living on the street these days. The fact reinforced her feeling that sometimes our culture could be so cruel and heartless. People were just not responding adequately to the problem of increasing poverty. There were times when Adrienne felt so lonely in this world, separated from people who shared her values. So much of the time she saw and read about repeated occurrences of abuse, some unintentional but a lot of it, such as violent crime, premeditated. It always made her feel so sad. Sometimes she wondered what she was doing on this planet. Those kinds of bleak thoughts made her reflect even more about herself and her purpose. She had always had a strong feeling that she had a destiny, something very special, but keeping the spirit of that concept alive was, on occasion, very difficult. Somehow she knew as difficult as that challenge was, that facing it was part of the destiny also.

Adrienne paid the cashier and left the store. Darkness had fallen while she had been in the supermarket. She began to push the cart along the bumpy parking lot toward her car. She noticed the street person was gone. Adrienne was disappointed; she had bought a bag of fruit to give to the homeless person. She approached the car and opened the trunk, put the bags inside and pulled the top down to slam it shut. As she slammed it down, she was startled to see someone standing on the side of the car. The person instantly took a step and stood next to her.

His face was covered with rags almost completely; just the eyes were showing through. They seemed to be shaped differently. Now shocked and frightened, she realized who it was.

"Shanta, you didn't heed my warning in Egypt."

This time she was better prepared. She held hope in her heart, and used it to push away the fear. His eyes shifted their stare for a moment.

"Oh, so you remember some of your lessons, little one. I can sense your pathetic attempt to protect yourself. You need much more to challenge me, but the thought of you trying to regain strength is amusing."

Suddenly her breath stopped.

"Pass through this life in an unassuming fashion, Shanta. If you don't and you choose to continue, I will take you to hell, slowly. While I would very much enjoy your slow decline, I assure you, you would find it torturous."

Adrienne felt as though her organs would burst; panic gripped her. The creature leaned toward her face his breath was so hot it seemed to burn her skin; her face felt seared.

"Accept defeat, or you will pray for it when I'm finished with you."

Then he was gone. Adrienne slid to the ground. Now able to breathe again, she took in several gasped gulps of air. Her head was spinning; she was so lightheaded. She just sat there trying to comprehend this frightening otherworldly experience.

She realized this thing that had watched her somehow had just assumed a street person's appearance. He had waited until it was dark to corner her, and then he seemed to just disappear. Either she had fainted or he just disappeared. If he did disappear that abruptly, he could not be human. The word that occurred to her was something she recalled from her college German class, Teufelgeist, demon ghost.

Her mind was reeling with this fact. He hadn't even touched her yet he was able to stop her from breathing. She suddenly just wanted to get away; away from there, away from him, or whatever it was. She was so afraid. Struggling to her feet, she leaned against the car for support. Her legs were weak, but her desire to escape was helping her to move. Adrienne wanted to be safe again, yet as she drove home she wondered if there was ever going to be a totally safe haven for her.

Hans was awakened by the shrill ring of the telephone. He fumbled for the receiver.

"Hello. Adrienne?

"Yes, it's me, Hans, I really hate to ask you, but could you come over and stay with me? I'm really scared."

"What's happened?"

"It's that man, or creature, whatever it is. The one in Egypt, remember?

"The one who threatened me. I've seen him again. I'm really frightened."

"Okay, I'll be there shortly."

Hans hung up the telephone. Sitting up on the side of the bed, he ran his fingers through his hair. Slowly getting up he sleepily walked to the closet to get some pants and a shirt. Slipping on his shoes, he walked into the bathroom and splashed cold water on his face. He walked toward the front door, grabbed his car keys and wallet, and slammed the door shut, hearing the lock engage as he left.

While driving through the dimly lit streets he began to become more lucid.

How could that guy from Egypt be here?

Maybe Adrienne was wrong; it really doesn't make sense. Yet, more he thought about it, several aspects of this entire experience were pretty unusual.

Hans began to remember his own past-life regression work. He was pretty surprised himself to learn about the threads of his history. The difference was he never really had a physical threat stemming from his regression work.

Who was this guy?

His car pulled up to Adrienne's apartment. His steps quickened as he approached the lobby. As the door opened, Hans was saddened to see how pale Adrienne looked.

"Adrienne, sit down. I'll make some tea. Have you eaten anything?"

She waved her hand to indicate that she had not eaten. She collapsed into a chair.

Hans set up a tray table, turned on the radio, and tuned into a classical music station. He made a ham sandwich and a cup of tea and brought them into Adrienne. He sat down on the couch and watched Adrienne sip at the tea, waiting until she finished eating the sandwich. Finally, he softly said,

"Adrienne, tell me what happened. Start from the beginning."

"Hans, it was him. He was watching me when I drove into the parking lot at the supermarket. I thought he was a street person. When I came out of the store, it was dark and all of a sudden he was there. He didn't really touch me, but he made my throat close up. I couldn't breathe."

She told Hans everything that had happened. Hans noticed her hands were shaking.

"What did he mean by 'your training'?" Hans asked.

"The regression work that Dr. Hart did showed that the group I belonged to worked with spiritual training. It must be that."

"Did you ever see him in your sessions?"

"No, not that I could detect from the tapes."

"Well, let's get you to bed. I'll bring in the television and that big chair. You lie down and I'll relax in the chair. We will talk to Dr. Hart about this mystery tomorrow."

Chapter Fourteen. Another Lifetime...

The sun was shining very brightly in the morning. Hans agreed to drive Adrienne to Dr. Hart's office and they arrived as soon as the secretary opened the door. Dr. Hart had not come in yet, so they sat in the reception area.

Adrienne could not help but notice and appreciate the beauty of the morning. What a contrast to the frightening experience she had so recently gone through. She felt much safer today. Distancing herself mentally from the danger she had been in was definitely improving her spirits.

Hans and Adrienne talked for a while and then Adrienne said,

"Hans, I know you must have many things to do, I feel as though I've held you up long enough."

Hans, looking into Adrienne's eyes, knowing how much he wanted to stay.

"If you don't mind me sitting in on the session, I would really prefer to stay with you."

"Well, I would love for you to stay. I really am still somewhat shaky from yesterday."

Together they walked into the session room. Dr. Hart was not there yet. His secretary said she expected him momentarily. Hans and Adrienne sat down again to wait. Adrienne tried to begin a lighter conversation.

"Hans, how is your book coming along?"

"Well, just a couple more chapters and I'll be finished. I'm really looking forward to completing the project. I've been working on this book for several years. The investment of energy, time and research, has really required a great commitment. So, as you can imagine, I'm definitely ready to put the final touches on the book and find a good publisher."

The office door opened. Dr. Hart and Gina walked in, Dr. Hart said, "Look what I found in the corridor."

Gina smiled and said hello. She always seemed so upbeat and enthusiastic.

"Wait until you see the results of my research!" she declared.

They all sat down in the regression lab. Gina spread out some photocopies of information she had obtained at the library.

"I was finally able to match more closely the inscriptions on the necklace we found on the young woman's skeletal remains. The inscription refers to a circle of people, a group that will remain joined through all time. Initially this group was formed centuries ago. Through tragedy, the group was temporarily broken up. They will regroup again through spiritual guidance after the harmonic convergence."

"When is that?" Adrienne asked.

Gina replied,

"Well, the majority of researchers seem to agree on Sunday, August 16, 1987 at sunrise. That would be the time that North American Indians and the Mayan culture seem to agree on as well. The energy emitting from the universe will shift and the planet Earth will go through a period of great increase in spiritual activity, a cleansing and a time to bring our troubled culture into more of a positive balance."

"This energy, will it just blanket the entire planet simultaneously", Adrienne asked.

"No, the initial focus was to be at sunrise around the ancient 'places of power': Stonehenge, Egypt, Mt. Shasta in California, the sacred wells in County Claire in Ireland, and several other areas."

Adrienne got up and walked to the window. She hoped to gain a sense of relief by staring out at the expanse of lawn outside the lab.

"Adrienne," Dr. Hart said while walking toward her, "what's wrong?"

"I just feel like we have so many unanswered questions. So many directions and no idea where we are going. And if we did will we ever get there? After last night's experience…that creature seems to have the power to kill me."

Dr. Hart was listening as Adrienne spoke about what had happened the previous evening and how afraid she was, suddenly Hans stood up and walked to the chalkboard in the lab.

"I think we do have much more of a defined direction if we look at the data from a different perspective."

Everyone watched as Hans began to verbally enumerate some of the facts. He began to write on the chalkboard as he spoke.

Facts

1. Psychic assaults from unknown negative influence increased

2. Chain and charm notations refer to grouping of nine and the chosen that will reunite

3. Identified Shanta as Adrienne

4. Part of the necklace found in tunnels in Egypt is an older, unidentifiable combination of metals

Questions

1. Why are the threats coming to Adrienne?

2. Where/Who are the nine?

3. How can we determine the meeting place?

4. What is the purpose of the meeting and how does it affect the world?

5. Who is this man/creature that is following Adrienne?

Everyone stared at the board. The room was completely quiet. Dr. Hart finally interrupted the silence.

"There is a part of this puzzle that is missing. We need to do another regression. Adrienne, we must see if the purpose and place of the meeting were explained to you by your mother in Egypt. Then, perhaps, we can understand who the threatening presence is, and why he is so determined to stop you. Adrienne, today we will try a different approach in the hypnotic regression work. I will regress you and then ask some specific questions. Perhaps we can find out if your mother gave you the answer to some of these questions about the group before she died."

Adrienne agreed to do the session, and they began immediately.

Moments later, Adrienne drifted into a deeply relaxed state with Dr. Hart's guidance.

She was in a dry, desert-like environment. Her clothing was a light cotton-like material that extended to her ankles.

"Rina."

"Yes, mother."

114

Rina touched her necklace which was made of smoothly shaped ivories with stone and turquoise shaded pieces. She liked the sounds they made as she moved. She walked outside the dome-shaped hut; it was huge. The people outside were all rushing about, carrying baskets, fruits, meats, breads. A strong spice scent filled the air; she could feel the excitement. Her mother's arm covered her shoulder.

"Come, Rina."

They began to walk together through the village, and people bowed respectfully to her as she passed them. They walked out past the village. The lake was nearby with large plateaus of stone surrounding different areas of the lake. Vines and flowers protruded from the rocks, drawing life from the water. Her mother stopped at one of those caves. Rina had been there many times to study. Her mother touched the wooden chimes hung at the mouth of the cave. The sounds of the wooden pieces ringing together were always pleasant to Rina's ear. Soon, Shosha appeared. She was very old, and greatly respected. Today, she was dressed in ceremonial garb. She was wearing an ivory- white, soft leather garment. Small, white feathers were attached to the ends of her hair in front. A large blue dot was in the center of her forehead. Rina knew from the teaching, Shosha had another internal eye, where the blue dot was located. Shosha could see much about people and the future using her third eye. Shosha left Rina's mother standing outside; she brought Rina into the cave. Shosha looked at Rina and said,

"Today is the day we have prepared for"

Rina knew what she meant and nodded. This was a special day. Shosha leaned toward her and pushed something on her forehead. Rina knew she now had a blue dot on her forehead, a third eye like Shosha's. Shosha pulled something from the bag she always wore about her neck. She put it on Rina. Rina's fingers touched the tiny pendant, upon which there were some inscriptions. She asked Shosha what this thing was.

"It is the future, your destiny, Rina. Remember we talked about how you will go ahead?"

"Yes, I remember."

"Well, this will help you remember when I am not with you."

"But Shosha, you said you were coming ahead also!" Rina said urgently.

"I am, and I will be there at the end, but for the little time we are apart, this pendant will guide you. I forged it myself according to the old laws. We will be together again. Do not worry, it will be. The time will be different, but you and I will meet here with the others in the circle. Never doubt. Come, we must go. Don't be afraid; I'm with you."

"Can we tell mother today, Shosha?"

"No, Rina. Most cannot live well with future sight. We cannot tell her. It would only be worse for her. Without the insight we have, her pain will be much less."

As they emerged from the cave, mother smiled. Rina knew how happy mother was, as she often said how proud she was of her. Shosha said that Rina must walk ahead and the rest would walk behind. Mother understood, and together they began their walk to the ceremonial grounds.

The grounds were covered with colored sands in various designs. As Rina grew closer to the center she could smell the strong scent of herbs burning. The scent made her somewhat lightheaded. She was placed in the center of the multicolored, multishaped circle. Shosha began to speak; the people grew silent.

"She is here, as foretold. The rest will join."

Slowly, from the crowd of people, eight other people came from all different directions. They assumed the same places where they had formerly stood. Each of these people was very special. Each had unique gifts of clairvoyance, psychic capabilities, energy healing and extra sensory perception.

They joined hands. All in the circle waited for Shosha to complete the link.

"The circle is complete; the chosen centered. As it was, it will be forever."

Soft chanting began. The moment was charged with energy, beauty and magic. All of the people circling the group could feel the beauty and positive energy emanating from the group. It made everyone feel so at ease and happy. A soft, glowing aura of light seem to pulsate from the entire area. A large bird circled overhead and began a loud, unceasing, screeching sound. Rina's eyes opened; she looked at Shosha. Shosha spoke in a whisper, "Rina, close your eyes. Use your mind flight as I've taught you. Separate your body and mind. You must trust in the teachings. I have put an herb into the ceremonial waters. The others will not feel much. Now, you must begin mind flight, Rina. You heard the bird, the time is here."

Shosha nodded her head for emphasis. Rina heard the hooves thunder. She looked up. At the top of the cliff she saw many horses, the one in front, the black horse was the leader. The rider's eyes were peering and appeared to flash an almost yellow color in the sun. He watched from above, and then suddenly the attackers seemed to be coming from everywhere. They had weapons. They were so frightening as they charged the onlookers. People began to scream in pain as they were attacked. Rina felt a numbing fear and horror in her mind. Shosha had foretold it, but to see this...Rina closed her eyes and made herself begin mind flight. The circle remained unbroken until death. Their spirits went forward, still joined even though the invaders hacked away at their lifeless bodies. Dr. Hart brought Adrienne out of her hypnotic state, with a suggestion that she would remember all that she had recalled from her past life.

Dr. Hart, Gina and Hans sat with Adrienne in a completely entranced fashion.

Gina was the first to break the silence.

"This is incredible. This revelation could change the whole concept of death as many people understand it. Adrienne somehow has an unbroken consciousness that has remained and is now brought forth into the present, with a mission to eventually join with people she was separated from back in the beginning of human time as we know it. If we can find these people and this place, their teachings would change the basic concepts of spirituality as many people know them today. It is such a..."

"Miracle," Adrienne finished the sentence.

"Yes, absolutely."

Gina went on,

"A miracle of life that these extraordinary capabilities have been given to humanity."

Adrienne hesitated, and finally spoke.

"They have been given to many. But that creature with the yellow-like eyes, he is the one I have seen in Egypt and again here. He also can transcend time and he wants me to stop, not to complete the circle. He doesn't want this gift to be returned to humanity through me. That's why he's trying to stop me."

Gina began thinking aloud,

"Positive and negative in the spiritual world. However, the story is told, the foundations are similar in that negative influences try very hard to maintain a hold on as many spirits as possible. A greater and widespread understanding of what some of these original teachers knew would increase the positive thoughts and behaviors in our world and decrease the negative. Therefore, an old soul with an evil philosophy would have a lot to lose."

Hans said,

"I can see why the harmonic convergence is such an appropriate beginning. Many of the current writings claim that there is too much negative influence is in our spiritual environment at this time. That negativity brings us closer to a destruction of some kind."

Dr. Hart began to speak,

"Well, obviously this, whatever he is, has been following Adrienne around for centuries. He has participated in her murder, and the murder of some of her family members and her teachers in past lives. If they had not had the gift of psychic sight and been vigilant, we would not even be discussing this now."

Adrienne finally spoke,

"We need to find the exact area for the meeting place. Dr. Hart, we will need to regress to see where I was; see if we can find it again."

Dr. Hart said,

"Not today, Adrienne. Enough excitement for you today, maybe tomorrow.

Let's recap what we know now. Initially, the setting seems to be somewhat desert-like; the plateaus of stone, etc. It is at least a drier, flatter place with areas of waterfalls clustered in rock groups. There are a lot of places we can begin to rule out. Hans, the groups you have worked with should be contacted. You should follow suit, Gina. See if we can find anyone who has been involved in past-life regression work with similar recollections. Obviously there are several other people on the planet who are in the same or similar situation as Adrienne. She is at the center of the group, but the rest of these people may be struggling to find answers."

Everyone agreed to meet the following day. Adrienne left and suddenly became aware that she was completely exhausted. All she wanted to do was take a hot bath, have a quiet dinner and forget all of the day's activities. Her mind felt overwhelmed by the implications of her role in this world.

Chapter Fifteen. Rina Guides the Group...

Adrienne woke up early, she had been tossing and turning most of the night. There were so many thoughts running through her mind. Fragments of memories had flashed in and out of her dreams. She sat on the side of her bed and decided to play one of her water sound tapes so she would relax while she prepared and ate breakfast. She put the coffee machine on and got some milk and cereal out to start her breakfast. She took her vitamins and sliced a banana for her cereal. She opened the door and picked up the morning newspaper and glanced at the front page as she sipped her coffee. Breakfast tasted good and she was feeling better already. She did some stretching exercises and rode her stationary bike for fifteen minutes. As she was heading for the shower, she began to look forward to her meeting with Dr. Hart.

Adrienne, feeling invigorated by her shower, heard the telephone ringing as she opened the bathroom door. She quickly grabbed the receiver, saying,

"Hello?"

"Adrienne, it's me, Hans. Good morning."

Adrienne was happy to hear his voice.

"Hi, good morning to you."

"Adrienne, I called to see if you wanted to meet me before we see Dr. Hart. Why don't we meet at the university coffee shop?"

"That would be fun. What time?"

"Well, how about 9:30 is that okay?"

"Great, I'll see you there. I've got to hurry and get dressed, so bye for now."

Adrienne quickly went to her closet as she decided what to wear. She realized she was trying to choose something flattering so that she would make a good impression on Hans. She was surprised at first to discover that her initial attraction to Hans had grown. As she thought about it, she realized that her life had been so crazy recently that she really hadn't had any time to think about her feelings regarding Hans or anything else. Reactive behavior had been dominating her decisions, and she usually liked more time to think and plan. As she finished dressing she looked in the mirror and said to her reflection,

"As soon as this whole mystery is solved, I will really begin planning my future."

She glanced at her watch and realized she had to hurry. Grabbing her keys, pocketbook and sweater, she ran for the door.

Hans was already sitting at a table with coffee waiting. He waved as she walked into the room. Spotting him right away, she walked quickly to the table.

"Hi!"

"Coffee light with sugar?"

"Right. You remembered?"

"I have a great capability to memorize things that are important to me."

He looked directly into her eyes. Adrienne was thinking how handsome he was. It was actually quite distracting for a moment as she searched for something to say.

"Do I fall into the category of 'important'?"

"Absolutely, Adrienne. We really have been spending so much time on the project that, well...I have a lot of things I've been thinking about that I haven't been able to tell you."

"Adrienne, I am attracted to you and I enjoy the time we've spent together. When this is over, I'd like for us to see each other a lot more. I think our relationship could really develop if we were able to focus on us."

Adrienne was flattered, and a little flustered.

"Han's I agree with everything you have said, and I think we should talk more about this and decide what to do. We can't really do that now, so maybe we can talk more at dinner?"

"Okay."

He responded.

His voice was filled with enthusiasm:

"This time, I'll cook my specialty, spaghetti with meatballs – with antipasto and Italian bread."

"Hans, you pick the time and I will be there, but now we've got to run. We have fifteen minutes to get to Dr. Hart's office."

Hans was surprised it was time to go, but agreed with Adrienne they should leave right away, he held her arm as he helped her up from her seat, wishing they could sit there and talk day.

Dr. Hart and Gina were already in the lab. They were anxious to begin work.

Soon Adrienne was in the reclining chair and Dr. Hart began the hypnosis. He directed her back in time, slowly through the centuries until she was Rina again. When he could begin, he asked her,

"What is the name of this place you live in?"

Her voice was slow to answer,

"Borda."

Dr. Hart said,

"Does that word have a meaning?"

"Where all lakes end."

"Rina, can you tell me why that name was given?"

"This is the last place that water flows before the sands begin."

"Sands. Do you mean the land is sandy and has no hills, no water at all?"

Her reply was again slow yet definite:

"Yes."

"Rina, tell me what color the land is in this sand place."

"By the mountains, almost like blood; the color gets lighter as it goes farther in the distance."

Dr. Hart had a charcoal pencil and pad.

"Rina, have you ever run your fingers in the sand to make shapes?"

"Yes."

"I would like for you to try to put those shapes down with this stick. Try and show how the lakes flow and where they end, and show how the mountains and the sand came together."

Adrienne sketched her recollections on the pad, from her time in history as Rina. When she was finished Dr. Hart thanked her and slowly withdrew the pad and pencil. He asked her to describe the weather.

"The sun is strong, when it is light outside. Sometimes we need to use the animal skins to cover ourselves at night."

Dr. Hart tried to find a term that could represent the change of seasons. Throughout the final questions he tried to elicit as much specific information as possible. The session was soon completed.

Adrienne awoke to Dr. Hart's voice quietly calling her name. As usual, she felt very relaxed, the room was still dark as the blinds were shut. Her eyes focused on the top of the window blinds, which slowly fluttered as a slight breeze came in through the small section of open window. Finally she spoke,

"Dr. Hart, were you able to find out the information we needed?"

"I think so."

He walked across the room, picking up the telephone to call his secretary and ask her to come in to pick up the tapes for transcription. Hanging up the receiver, he sat on the edge of the desk. Thinking for a moment, he looked at Adrienne, and said

"Well, we can get the latest information transcribed, typed out and entered into the system for analysis within the hour. If we can get an update from Hans and Gina we will have information on possible locations, and individuals. In addition, identifying people who may have had regression hypnosis that revealed experiences in a similar environment would be very helpful. Perhaps some correlation of their reflections, including any tribal experience and religions similar to the group you were with at the time of physical death. I have also contacted other agencies I have had trusted relationships with, and Hans and Gina have networked with groups they have confidence in, so we will have our research culminating in some very qualified leads."

Adrienne stretched, saying,

"I'm going to take a break, take a walk or something. When do you need me back?"

Glancing at his watch, he seemed to ponder for a moment.

"How about three hours? You'll have time for lunch and a nice break."

"Great, I'm going to do some shopping. I received a check for one of the articles I wrote and I think I'll buy myself a new outfit or something fun."

Dr. Hart laughed he said,

"Adrienne, you never cease to amaze me. You always keep such a balanced and positive outlook. Our schedule has really put you under a lot of pressure and some of the experiences you have had have been traumatic. Somehow, you are managing all of this very well."

Adrienne looked up at Dr. Hart. She was slightly flushed; the compliment was so unexpected it had made her blush.

"Thanks, I appreciate the encouragement," she paused,

"Somehow it reassures me. I may act well balanced, but I must admit, it has been quite a struggle some days. I made myself persevere to get to the final answer and solve, once and for all, this puzzle that has been my life. Ever since I was young, I've looked like other people but I had experiences so different from them. Even though I'm excited about our progress, I'm scared, too. Thanks for the support."

Shyly standing by the door, she opened it up and looked at Dr. Hart.

"Well, I'll see you later. Bye."

The secretary passed her on the way in. Dr. Hart waved at Adrienne and she walked briskly down the hall toward the parking lot.

Adrienne got into the car; it was sunny, a great day. She decided to go to her favorite shopping mall and look for a new outfit to wear on her dinner date with Hans. When she pulled into the parking lot, she found a spot close to the mall entrance right away. She locked the car, walked to the escalator and, when she emerged from the underground garage, her eyes glanced up at the cascading shower that dominated the front area of the shopping mall. She walked directly toward the waterfall and stood watching the multitude of streams flowing over the rock wall. At the bottom, there were several artfully shaped pools and rocks built around them to keep the water flowing downward. Soothing gurgling sounds filled the entire area. Ferns and flowered plants were tastefully arranged in and around the waterfalls. It was truly a beautiful sight.

Adrienne sat on a marble bench and watched as two little children threw shiny pennies into the little streams. They giggled and hugged each other with excitement over the splashes that the coins made as they tossed them into the water. They were absolutely beautiful children, with golden curls sweeping around their faces as they jumped up and down. They were perspiring slightly from all of their activity and some of the curls around their foreheads were slightly damp and spiraled even more tightly. Adrienne smiled; the children's laughter was wonderful to hear. The children's mother finally called for them.

"Come on now, time to go."

She slowly led them away. Adrienne realized that almost a half-hour had passed. She began to walk toward the shops. She walked into one of the women's clothing shops. She was immediately drawn to one outfit; it was a matching skirt and blouse. It looked great on her so she purchased it and went to the shoe store across the walkway. She was definitely having exceptionally good shopping luck. She found shoes that fit, matched her outfit and were reasonably priced. She thought about

heading home and began walking toward the exit to find the car.

Chapter Sixteen. New Directions...

As she walked down the shopping mall corridor, she noticed a large poster by the elevator. There was a woman who was a famous psychic and channeler here today. She was to be interviewed by some Television talk show host. The poster said they were at a large book store at the front section of the mall. Apparently the psychic had written a book and was doing a book signing session, combined with a Television interview. Adrienne decided to walk toward the area just to see what was happening.

She saw a small crowd of people, most of whom were sitting on metal folding chairs. A platform had been erected and two cameramen were taping everything. The female talk show host was walking among the people seated, asking for volunteers. As she reached the end of the aisle, she was standing in front of Adrienne.

"Hi, my name is Joan Smythe. And your name?"

Adrienne was surprised that the woman had spoken to her, and then gave her name to the show's host.

"Adrienne, we are going to have a woman on the show today who is a psychic and channels information. Would you feel comfortable asking her a question or two?"

Adrienne had thought of her visit as a brief observation as opposed to active participation. Then she thought,

"Oh, why not?"

"Sure, Joan, that would be fine; it should be interesting." She said.

"Okay. Five minutes before we begin. Scotty, please get Adrienne a name tag and a chair in the front."

Adrienne settled in her chair, filled with curiosity. The show began; Joan introduced Santee.

"Santee has been channeling for the public for five years now, and has already been tested at several universities and confirmed to have a very high degree of psychic power. Santee, there are so many people in our audience who are curious about what channeling is. Could you talk a little about that experience?"

"Joan, I had been studying toward a degree in metaphysics and working with a psychic instructor developing my psychic abilities for ten years. One weekend, while on a retreat, I began to get responses to questions, either my own or other people's inquiries, with help from a spirit guide. These answers were from a source outside of myself, and basically flowed through me. I was able to help people with questions that they had about current problems, health issues a variety of things that made a great difference in people's lives. I have continued to do that work ever since that time."

"Thank you and Santee"

Joan turned to the audience saying,

"Let me inform the people here today that Santee has an established clientele that come to her for guidance, and she has worked with the Federal Bureau of Investigation, Smithsonian Institute, missing children's groups, and several police departments with great success in nearly every case. Her most recent book explains more about her work and the techniques she uses to help people. I have some people here today with questions. Sharon?"

A petite, attractive woman stood up. Big brown eyes with a sad cast to them glanced at the psychic.

·

"My husband passed away after a long and painful illness. Can you tell me if he is at peace now?"

Santee thought for a moment. The woman in the audience was so sad her eyes filled with tears and she was unable to speak.

"My guide tells me Bill has seen your sorrow and wants you to have a happy life, not to mourn for him. He is content; he says to remind you to look at the inscription that you have inside your wedding band. 'Together, Forever' He will always be by your side and does not want you to live your life in mourning."

Tears streamed down the young woman's face. She smiled and sat down shaking her head in wonder. Joan walked to the next person. Adrienne looked at him; his nametag said 'Tim' He stood up; he was about six feet tall, blond, blue-eyed and slender. Dressed in business attire, he seemed somewhat embarrassed to be participating in a group question-and-answer session. Santee spoke,

"I can see the question on your mind is private. Suffice to say you were wrong in your suspicion. There is no need for any concern."

Tim's lower jaw dropped a little bit. He was surprised and relieved. He thanked her and sat down.

Now it was Adrienne's turn. She stood up and looked at Santee. Santee began to speak.

"I get a psychic sense of your inquiry. You are an older spirit, with a great responsibility. Your direction affects humankind. You have a powerful enemy. You will be more powerful; you will succeed. You begin the circle. Does that resonate with you?"

Adrienne nodded yes.

"We will talk again at a later time."

Adrienne was really at a loss for words. Finally she said, "Thank you."

She sat down, quite amazed at this person's capabilities.

Lost in thought and unaware that the show was finished, she felt a slight touch on her shoulder. Adrienne turned to see the channeler's face. Her eyes, like almond-colored pools, reflected a kindly, relaxed expression.

"Shall we have some tea?"

"Yes."

Adrienne welcomed the company and hoped for further clarification of Santee's earlier comments. They began to walk away together. Adrienne realized she was now hungry and ordered a salad with the tea. As she began to eat, Adrienne asked Santee how she first knew about her abilities and how they developed.

"When I was a child, I used to have dreams. Spirits would tell me things about questions that my relatives had. The spirits appeared in my dreams and would ask me to relay the message to the inquiring person. My mother was somewhat psychic and apparently would pray and direct her questions to relatives who had passed on. On some of the more serious issues, spirits would try and relay responses for her through me. I did not even begin to understand any of this and did not give it a lot of thought. When I was older the communication increased to my wakened state and if people asked questions, very frequently I channeled responses. When I was in my early twenties, I met a woman in her eighties; she was a channeler as well. She became my mentor and trained me, showed me meditation techniques, circle protection, and assisted me in developing my concentration so I could have a stronger relationship with my spirit guides."

"Santee, you mentioned an enemy of mine. Could you help me understand that more through the intervention of your spirit guides?"

"Adrienne, they choose when and how much to tell me, and I shared that information with you today. I would certainly be happy to help you though, I can sense your burden is a very difficult one."

Adrienne looked at the daisies in the center of the table and touched the soft petals.

"Well, I didn't realize it when I was younger, but the experiences I am having have dominated a lot of my life. I've understood a little more as I got older, as you did. I'm working with a specialist in the field of exploration of past lives. Finally, a lot of answers are coming together to help me understand fully what has been happening."

Santee said,

"I feel your destiny is a critical one. I would like to help you in any way I can."

A perky young woman approached the table with the check pad and pen in her hand. "Can I get you anything else?"

"No, thank you; we are all set."

Adrienne reached for the check and quickly said,

"My treat. I know you have a busy schedule. It was nice of you to spend the time with me."

Santee looked up quickly, and said,

"You don't have to thank me. I am very pleased we met."

As they walked to the parking lot, Adrienne asked Santee if she would like to meet Dr. Hart. Adrienne had an intuitive sense that Santee should be part of the work the team was doing. Santee agreed to meet Adrienne at Dr. Hart's office the next morning.

Adrienne drove back to Dr. Hart's office, feeling absolutely great. She wanted to tell Dr. Hart of her meeting with Santee, and how she just felt intuitively that Santee could help the work the group was doing. She knew when Dr. Hart met her he would see that her channeling abilities would be wonderful to be able to work with. Adrienne found herself singing part of an old Carole King song,

"I feel the earth move under my feet."

Where was she recalling that song from?

She pondered

Adrienne began to remember, it was about ten years ago when she had that apartment on the hill. Life was so different. She had those awful reoccurring dreams back then. Now, so many of those troubling experiences had been explained through her work with Dr. Hart.

It made her feel good to have gained some control and understanding of these experiences. She continued pondering for a moment and realized she was also somewhat frightened of some aspects of this newfound clarity in realizing that as she came closer to some answers, her progress brought her closer to danger.

Chapter Seventeen. The Future Unfolds...

The group sat in a circle. They had decided to try working together in a focused session – Dr. Hart, Hans, Santee, Adrienne, Ona and Gina. Santee asked for a few minutes of meditation time, to begin contact with her guide. In the silence Adrienne heard her own heart beating. She was confident that Santee's channeling would really help her. Hans seemed to sense her feelings. When their eyes met, he nodded slightly and smiled to encourage her. Santee began to speak.

"Adrienne, as the leader you must go to Asharte, now called Guatemala. That's where the attack occurred. After the attack, the few survivors remaining left the area and went to the area known as the Yucatan Peninsula. The Mayans had settled in the area and an amazing culture flourished. You will find some of these souls waiting in Asharte and more waiting in the Yucatan. Six, including you, are now in the room, they are part of the ten that is to be reunited. The circle of ten is destined to reunite in September of this year. There will be a solar eclipse, a new beginning for the sun, and a new moon cycle on the same day. It is foretold that the circle of the sun and the moon will meet at the crossroads of winds and the universe will be rejoined. The change will then be complete, that which had already begun with the harmonic convergence."

There was a long silence. Adrienne finally spoke.

"Santee, who are the souls in this room that you referred to?"

Santee said,

"Ona, Gina, Dr. Hart, Hans. You and I are among them.

"Your guide and teacher, Shosha, is with you in spirit now and will be in flesh to you, in the very near future."

Slowly Santee looked up; she was visibly drained. Dr. Hart offered her the reclining chair they used for hypnosis so that she could rest. Gina went to the refrigerator to get her some juice. Everyone in the room marveled as they listed to the tape recording of the session.

Things were so much clearer now. Adrienne now understood why she had felt so close to Hans. Hans now had the remaining piece to his own regression work and Ona's evidence was confirmed.

Plans for the journey began immediately. They had to be there within the time frame Santee had told them about. Everyone took a role in the coordinating of the plans. There was a lot to do and time was of the essence. Departure would be in twenty-four hours. Santee would not join them at this point of the trip, as she had a prior commitment, so they said their goodbyes. Everyone agreed to meet at the airport. Hans and Adrienne had made dinner plans days ago to find some time to discuss their relationship, so they left together to pick up airline tickets.

Hans and Adrienne had been seated at the windowed section of the restaurant. The view was spectacular. The sun was setting, casting an orange glow across the bay and reflecting on the sailboats and yachts docked at the marina. It was a beautiful sight.

In the adjoining room someone was playing a relaxing tune on the piano. Hans and Adrienne had both agreed that the lobster had been delicious.

"Dessert?"

Hans asked and looked over at Adrienne.

"Well, let's check the menu. If we see something really tempting, we can share it. I don't think I could eat an entire dessert."

"Chocolate mousse",

they said at the same time, and laughed. Hans signaled the waiter and ordered dessert to be served with two spoons.

They decided after dinner to walk out on the balcony overlooking the ocean. Walking arm in arm along the deck they spotted a bench and sat down.

"This is really beautiful, don't you think?"

Adrienne asked and looked at Hans.

He just stared at her for a moment. Finally he said,

"You look beautiful. While I'm on the subject, this may come as a surprise to you, but I think I've fallen in love with you. We've been so busy with the project and you have had so much personal difficulty to deal with, we haven't been able to discuss this. I know we have a lot going on right now, but…"

"Hans," Adrienne stopped him, "I'm glad you told me. But, I will be in great danger in the very near future. I don't even know if I will live. As much as I care deeply for you, it could be a mistake to become more seriously involved right now."

Adrienne looked at Hans. He stared at her for a moment then said,

"I'll take the risk."

Their lips met. Adrienne was not aware of any other thought at that moment. She realized she loved Hans, and whatever time they had left they would spend it together.

Chapter Eighteen. Ashtarte…

Finally, the journey had begun, the heat was intense. The trip to Egypt had certainly helped them prepare for walking in the sun: learning to wear light colors, drinking plenty of fluids, staying in the shade as much as possible, and taking frequent breaks from walking. Unfortunately, the burros were not as fast as the camels had been. The travelers could see a group of small adobe huts in the distance. Everyone agreed to stop for a siesta there. The sun would be at its peak, so resting for those two hours would be wise.

Ona and Dr. Hart rode ahead to see if they could find someone who would rent them some rooms to rest in, and a barn for the burros. Their guide and translator pointed out some areas of interest to Adrienne and Hans as they approached the village. Apparently gold had been mined in the area and several dilapidated mining buildings leaned precariously against the low part of the mountain range. Adrienne commented how dry and dusty the land was.

"How do you grow any food here?"

The old man's eyes shifted the gaze he had been holding and looked at Adrienne.

"My ancestors tell me this was a beautiful land, with crops in the shade of the mountains and trees so large that homes were built in and around them. Then the struggle began. People with no conscience came and took from the land and the people, took gold, took lives, never giving back to anyone or anything. The land shriveled from their selfishness. We cannot grow much because the basic law was broken. It is said someday all will be restored."

Adrienne inquired about where the water had come from before the change.

"Between the two peaks," he said pointing toward the old town. Adrienne looked. Above the old town were two towering hills. "The guardians watch over the source."

"The guardians?" Adrienne asked.

"Yes, there is a group born to this; each generation trains the next."

"What are they supposed to do?"

He stopped his burrow and the guide stared at her for a long time.

"Not many are as interested as you are, and as I look at you, I see a strong resemblance in your face to a sketch I've seen. This might seem like a strange question, but may I ask if you have a mark under your arm that you were born with?"

Haltingly, Adrienne said,

"Yes, I do."

"You must come with me after your siesta."

The guide said,

"To see the guardians. Will you come?"

"Can I bring my companions?"

"Yes."

The guide said quickly,

"of course"

"But you must come to visit the guardians."

Adrienne felt as though she very much wanted to visit these guardians, although she didn't know why. She decided she would follow her intuition and see them.

The village they entered to rest in was in poor condition. Buildings were low and cracked with age and, combined with the incessant heat, had quickly fallen to ruin. The streets were strangely empty. Most inhabitants were already indoors for siesta. Dr. Hart was directing the group toward one of the dwellings. Adrienne felt such a relief upon entering. It was dark and much cooler. The wooden shutters had been pulled across all the windows to keep in the cool air of the morning and protect against the intensity of the midday sun.

As her eyes adjusted to the dimness, she could see a table set with mugs and a pitcher.

The room was very homey looking; the couch and floor were covered with beautifully colored hand woven mats. The reds, oranges and yellows were so clear and vibrant; a lovely contrast to the whitewashed walls. The wood around the fireplace was polished and had a deep shine. Handmade clay tiles with symbols that looked like scenes from nature were tacked neatly around the edges of the fireplace.

Dr. Hart interrupted her observations.

"Adrienne, would you like some juice?"

"Yes, I'm really thirsty. It's so hot outside."

As Dr. Hart passed out glasses of juice, the group began to talk. Dr. Hart explained to everyone,

"We will have cots to rest on and after our siesta we will have some lunch provided for us."

A woman came around the corner to guide them to their rooms. The interpreter explained to her and the group he would be back later after their siesta. Ona was also bi-lingual, so if anyone needed anything in his absence she could help. Everyone picked up their backpacks, and walked to their rooms to rest. Adrienne shared a room with Ona. Dr. Hart and Hans were directed to a separate area. Adrienne was delighted to see a large bowl and pitcher of water which she could use to freshen up. She took off her blouse and shorts and sprinkled water on her face, arms and legs. Patting herself dry with the linen towel, she felt so much more comfortable with the traveling dust removed from her body. She stretched out on the cot and drifted off to sleep immediately.

Adrienne seemed lost in the fog. She really couldn't see anything at all. She groped along, feeling her way through what seemed to be a rocky cave.

"Where am I?"

Her voice echoed throughout what sounded like a never-ending cavern.

She continued to feel her way along the wall. She noticed pictures, drawings on the side of the wall; they seemed to be hand-painted. There were symbols representing birth, life and death, all depicted in intricate circles. Suddenly she heard a horrible scream, a woman's scream. Adrienne turned her head in an attempt to figure out where it had come from, but the sound stopped. Then she heard the sound of drums, a low, monotonous drumbeat that got louder as she slowly felt her way along the wall. Adrienne felt as if she were turning a corner. In the distance, she could see a glow of firelight. While she was walking toward the fire, another scream pierced her ears. It was so frightening she dropped to the ground. Frantically looking around, she tried to see through the haze of smoke. The screaming abruptly stopped and became a gurgle.

Adrienne crawled along the wall toward the fire. She was about fifteen or twenty feet away from it, but the haze was so thick she could not see clearly. She slowly stood up, pressing herself against the wall to remain as hidden in the shadows as possible. She remained frozen in that position, watching for some movement around the flames.

She was trying to see what had happened, and figure out whom those screams has come from.

The haze blew away in the blink of an eye. She now had clear sight and the view froze her against the wall.

"Adrienne, I've been waiting for you."

It was he; his yellow, strangely-shaped eyes seemed to burn through the darkness. He spoke in some strange lost language, that she had not heard in this life, and yet she could understand him. She felt her arms being pulled. She looked up and saw two serpent-like men on each side of her, dragging her toward their master. They drooled on her arms as they walked. She wondered if this was a dream.

It must be! This could not be real.

He sat on a throne carved into the side of the cave. On each side of him were two stakes in the ground with women tied against the wood, both with their throats slashed open. Blood was dripping into an underground waterfall. Mist from the huge waterfall bubbled up and around everyone. It was hot and made the smell of the blood almost overpowering. The serpent men shoved her to her knees.

"Know your place as my servant, Adrienne. That is the name you are called in this life, is it not?"

He began to laugh. Adrienne could not speak.

"Answer me!"

His scream resounded in her head. She nodded weakly, watching the blood drip everywhere. She was faint with fear.

"Why have you come? You've had revelations of our past together, so surely you are not coming to challenge me again. Did you not learn on the plains of the Asharte? Do you need another reminder? Shall I kill your entire group again, just as I've taken these souls?"

He gestured to the two bodies tied to the stakes beside him.

"They would have tried to help you, but no more. Save yourself for once, and spare the others around you, if you value them. This will be your last chance, Adrienne. Our next meeting will result in your death. This time you will not escape me. I will possess you and, through you, countless others until the end of time."

His eyes seemed to bore into hers as he uttered his threat.

She awoke with a start. Ona was speaking,

"Adrienne, are you all right...? It's okay, you were just dreaming."

Adrienne mumbled,

"More than a dream he will kill all of us."

She told Ona what happened, how she had seen him before and now he was giving her a final warning.

"Adrienne, there must be something protecting you that we don't understand. He could have killed you there, but he couldn't touch you. It's as if he's trying to frighten you into stopping because it seems that he cannot do it by himself."

Adrienne stood up and looked out at the desert. Her eyes scanned the landscape. There was definitely some logic to what Ona had said. It never had occurred to her to consider that viewpoint. He had always been such a fearful opponent. Clearly that is what he wanted, to use her fear to do the work, because obviously he had never been able to eradicate her spirit, despite centuries of effort.

"Ona, you are so wise! I am still intimidated by this enemy, but your insight gives me a sense of clarity that I did not have before. I need to think about this some more, but we have to meet the others. Let's collect our things and get started."

Bidding farewell to their kind hosts, the group departed. Riding in a single file, the party and their guide began the final leg of the journey to the next village and then to the site in the Yucatan.

The village seemed abandoned as they approached it. The ride had been long, dusty and hot. Adrienne felt as though everything on her was covered with a fine, powdery, reddish clay dust. Her eyes scanned the village for some sign of humanity. A dog began to bark in the distance.

"Surely someone must live here?"

She directed her question to the guide. He had stopped his mule and, looking up and down, he seemed a little perplexed.

"Is something wrong?" Adrienne asked worriedly.

The guide tipped his face toward her; the sun shining in tiny droplets across his weathered face through his old straw hat.

"It is unusual that more people are not about. Siesta is finished for today. I think we should pull the animals into the barn. I have known the owners for years; I am sure they will not mind."

Once inside the barn, out of the direct sun, Adrienne felt a little cooler. There was a large leather bag hanging from the barn wall. It was full of liquid. The guide took it down and began to pass out water to everyone. Adrienne felt that she had never had such refreshing water. The ride had been so hot and dry that the drink provided an incredible relief.

She looked around at Hans, Dr. Hart and Ona. Everyone's face seemed to express the puzzlement that she felt.

Once everyone was settled, the guide agreed to see if he could find someone who knew what was going on. He went to open the barn door. As it creaked open, two children ran by quickly. They were shouting as they ran. The guide shouted a greeting to them. Both children were startled but they quickly recognized his face. They exchanged words, the children jumping and pointing to the opposite end of the town. The guide thanked them and they ran off.

"Apparently, two women have been hurt. The children could only see a little of the scene. The adults would not let them get close enough and quickly sent them home. I will go and see what has happened. Sit down and rest here in the shade. I will be back soon."

Hans came over to Adrienne, putting his arm around her. He whispered,

"Are you okay?"

She felt better with Hans hugging her.

"Hans, I am going to be so relieved when all of this is over. I have never had so much tension and fear in my life. It really is so good to have you with me. I've really begun to rely on you. I can't tell you how much it means to me."

Hans looked into her eyes, saying,

"Adrienne, it really has come to mean a lot to me also. I have really begun to care for you, more than I realized. I think we should…"

The barn door was abruptly opened. Everyone's gaze shifted toward it. The guide came in looking very troubled.

"There have been two murders; two women are dead."

Dr. Hart asked what happened to them.

"Their throats were cut."

Adrienne stood up and said,

"I must see them. Can you take me? In my dream there were two women in a cave. They were killed the same way."

The guide looked at her saying,

"You are the one. I knew it. You have the sight."

He thought for a moment, then said,

"All right, we will go, but only you. The people in the village are already so upset by this tragedy that all of us going would be a mistake. Reverence for the dead must be observed."

Quickly, Adrienne walked out the door. The ground was so dry. She looked down at her shoes as she walked. Pebbles and stones were sprinkled about. Her foot slipped on some of the larger stones as she hurried. Her thoughts were disrupted as the old guide touched her arm. He gestured toward the door.

"In here," he whispered.

They both turned and walked through a stone entrance to an old chapel. It felt very cool inside. Adrienne could not really see in the darkness. The sun had been so bright that her eyes took a few moments to adjust. Six or seven people were standing around two long tables. They all looked up at her. The eldest woman stepped away from the table as if to approach the visitors. Adrienne could see the two slain women; their throats had indeed been ripped open. They were the same women in what she had previously assumed was her dream. But, this was no dream. Her eyes were trained on the bodies, she was horrified at what she saw. Everything began to spin; she felt shaky. Her eyes seemed to flutter. She reached out her hand and felt a strong grip on her arm as she collapsed.

The elder, who was called Asha, had Adrienne's limp body carried to the nearest pew. She called for a cool cloth and some water. She wiped Adrienne's forehead gently. As she wiped her neck and arms, she saw the birthmark. Everyone was standing watching as Asha tended to Adrienne. A slight gasp was heard from two of the others. Asha looked up and nodded. No one needed to speak. It was understood who the visitor was, they were in the presence of the chosen one.

They had been preparing for this moment for centuries. That it had finally arrived was a welcome miracle. Their lives would now be changed forever. The world would change as well. Everything hinged on "The Chosen."

Adrienne's eyes fluttered open.

"What happened?" She mumbled.

She saw the elder's face and felt her gentle, soothing touch.

"Rest. You will be fine." Asha assured.

Adrienne believed her immediately. Her eyes began to scan the wall. She could now see the ancient symbolic drawings that made up the border of the top of the windows. They looked like stick figures and the sun and moon. The drawings surrounded the entire chapel. Her observations were interrupted as Asha sat down with her.

"I am Asha. I am the head of the elders. Some call us the guardians. She paused and spoke slowly,

"You...are 'The Chosen'. We have waited here for generations to join you."

Adrienne looked into the woman's eyes.

"You know of me?"

The elder looked into Adrienne's eyes, declaring...

"You will change the world. This has been taught since the beginning of our time. It is written on our walls here from the drawings left by our ancestors in the caves. The story is all there. We are to help with the final circle."

Adrienne interrupted Asha, asking,

"Where is the final circle to be? Do you know?"

"It is here." Asha responded.

The elder pulled up Adrienne's arm, pointing to the birthmark.

"You see?" She pointed to the symbol on the top of the chapel. "The birthmark is a map. The larger map you can see on the wall. The shape is the canyon where the circle was broken centuries ago. The circle will meet again very soon."

Adrienne slowly sat up. She could not believe that she was hearing the woman talk so knowledgeably about something that for years she had not fully understood, and sometimes had even doubted her own sanity for considering. She and Asha walked to the wall drawing. The guide spoke quickly.

"I know this place very well. We can be there tomorrow."

The elder spoke to Adrienne,

"Look at the wall. You see? The story shows you came with some of our circle. You'll meet some people here and the rest in the canyon. That is the circle site. Your final destination is one of the sacred places. A space of reverence. Temples that were built by the great Mayans."

"First, we must bury our sisters. Then we can go with you. You may join in the burial service if you would like, Adrienne. In fact, they were your sisters, too; as you can see, everyone in this group has been connected together for all time."

The burial was attended after sunset by the entire village, as well as a large gathering of people from surrounding areas. The word had spread quickly during the day, after the women had been discovered outside a large cave at the base of the twin peaks. Circles were formed around the grave site and handmade linens had been prepared for the dead. The elders of the tribe led the prayers and chants to bid these souls farewell on their journey. When the ceremonies were completed, the group filed back to the chapel and the deaths were recorded in an ancient log inside the chapel chamber.

The guide approached Adrienne and Asha, and told them that the guardians would like to sit with them in the meeting lodge. Fortunately Asha had been schooled in basic English as a child in a church on the edge of town. She would be able to translate for Adrienne when they met with the group. Asha took Adrienne's arm and began to walk with her toward the lodge. Adrienne somehow felt it was quite natural that this woman should be guiding her. The recollection of her regression tapes returned and she realized this was most assuredly Shosha, her teacher and spiritual guide of long ago.

As the group assembled, Adrienne felt this process of meeting in a circle of elders was very comfortable and somehow familiar to her. The group now assembled together and Asha began to speak.

"She is here. She has the mark," Asha said holding up Adrienne's arm. She revealed the birthmark so the group could get a closer view.

"It shows us the place of the circle. The day of our meeting is upon us. We will start the journey tomorrow. I will go and some among you will be coming to help with our journey. If the powers be with us, we will return in safety. Our world will be changed for the better as we have hoped and prayed for generations. As you know, the danger is an old one. The evil power is strong, and has killed many to use their fear. He has been able to take human form in this way. You will have to assemble as a group and pray over us on our journey, and, most especially, for the circle. Let's join hands one last time before we go."

As the group joined hands, the room became quiet. Adrienne could feel love, trust and peace. Beautiful visions formed in her mind. A sunny day, people in white linen forming a circle, the people all seemed so kind and happy. She rested, watching that scene. When she opened her eyes, she was surprised to see a glow of energy that illuminated the modest, structure. The group of people was emanating energy that radiated. How amazing; Adrienne had never seen such a thing! Each person seemed transformed, their faces content, no longer showing lines of age or worry. Asha spoke,

"This is the power that will be helping to guide and support us on this dangerous journey. We are fortunate to have the power of ages handed down to our group by the elders before us."

Slowly, the guardians arose from their sitting positions, then hugged and the travelers said goodbye and departed to their homes.

The next morning it was agreed that Asha and Adrienne would go to the sacred site alone to spend some time there. The guide would take Dr. Hart, Ona, Hans, Santee and the others to the meeting place. They would all ultimately meet at the meeting site at the outskirts of the circle site. It was beginning to be very hot, even though they had started out early in the morning to try and avoid some of the high temperatures. Asha said,

"We will travel east to the city."

Adrienne asked how they would find some of the others that belonged to the circle. Asha smiled,

"I know of them, not to worry. We have sent word to the tribal elders that we are on the way to the village."

They walked in silence, each pondering the future. Adrienne fought the occasional tremors of fearfulness. She trusted in her heart that the power of this group would prevail. However, the reality of the negative influence that threatened her and tried to diminish her own power was troubling. She now knew more about her enemy's strategy. She then recalled her own strength, the depth of which was great, this power that had spanned generations. Her ability to manifest this strength was so far reaching. She had maintained the courage to persist in her learning and she had uncovered secrets beyond her imagination. This is part of what the struggle had been about. Her enemy tried to keep her in shadows of ignorance, in a valley of despair, to use her own fear against her as a weapon. Adrienne understood she was pitted against a cunning enemy who manipulated people to cause them to struggle against themselves. By keeping them distracted by their internal fear and doubt, they would never get a glimmer of their true potential.

Evening was approaching. Adrienne thought her eyes were playing tricks on her at first, but saw there were lights ahead.

"Asha, what is that ahead?"

"We approach the village. The moon celebration is tonight. The tribes have gathered."

Adrienne looked ahead. The stars began to show through the dark blue sky. Now the deep purple outline of the hills was barely visible. The fires that had been lit were brighter and burned very high. She could see hot sparks spit and lift from the flames flying up like fireflies.

As they approached the tribal fire sites, Adrienne began to see that many groups had come together like a rainbow of colors. The sight was breathtaking. The first group she saw wore all black and white tribal colors. The lead person in their circle dance was tall and strong in his stance and steps. His black hair was long and straight under an elaborate feather headdress and the carefully matched feathers, alternately black and white, covered the entire length of his body. His movements mimicked that of a tall, proud bird. In vigilant movements that suggested an awareness of attack, he strutted around to each standing member of the circle.

Adrienne was transfixed by the beauty and power of this experience. Her eyes continued to travel, stopping to see another group in a line procession. Each person in this group had a different style of dress. The feathers used were from many different birds, all colors, and arranged in many styles. The cloaks people were wearing were dyed to match. The first man in line had warrior paint in bold red slashes across his face. His cloak was woven wool held with a silver clasp with a round crystal in the center. He had ornate suede boots with multicolored beads woven in a pattern across the top. As the low vibrations of the drum sounded, his movements matched the tempo of the music. It was hypnotic to observe in person. Adrienne felt suspended in time, as though everything else had stopped for this celebration.

Suddenly, she felt the warmth of a soft cloak on her shoulders. It felt so comforting. She looked to her side and saw a young woman in the formal dress of her tribe. She had unusually piercing blue eyes of such a deep color, Adrienne was transfixed. Adrienne felt those eyes could peer directly into her consciousness. It felt as though this woman knew her, knew her well; all her thoughts, past and future. The woman spoke, breaking what seemed like a long silence.

"We have known each other in another time. In this time I am called Nasha. I knew you were coming so I made this for you, much like the one you used to wear when you were very young."

Adrienne, puzzled, now glanced around her shoulder. The cloak, dyed a deep red, was decorated on the trim, heavily beaded in many colors of beads and turquoise inlay. In the back of the cloak, long, white smooth feathers neatly formed a V-shape. Each side had small, white fluffy feathers that formed a long, continuous border down each side. As Adrienne's gaze returned forward, the young woman connected a clasp which was made of silver with a round crystal at the center. As Adrienne looked up she saw the lead male in the first tribal line approach her. Nasha spoke,

"That is Meha."

In his hand was a headdress of short, smooth white feathers with a smaller round crystal at the front of the headpiece.

"The time grows near. Are you ready?"

His voice was deep, yet familiar in some way. She knew what he meant by his comment. She nodded and he slowly placed the headdress on her. She was ready and knew the fight of her life would soon take place.

The moon was almost completely full. It seemed so close, so much larger out here in this open landscape. Adrienne looked at what appeared to be shadows in the surface of the moon. She wondered how long the moon had actually existed.

She knew it had been there through all of the lifetimes she had recalled in her work with Dr. Hart. The moon had survived and guided many; she hoped this would be her fate, as well. She trembled slightly with anticipation and some fear. The tribes danced below, offering their energy through this ritual. Ceremonies at this full phase of the moon would assist their cause. As the moon waxes toward being full, so the powers of affirmations increase. Seeing the large numbers of people who had assembled for this occasion reminded Adrienne how many people's spiritual and physical existence hinged on the upcoming confrontation. The circle would form again and her belief was strong that this time it would not be broken.

The circle. Her mind went back in time, recalling her original group of spiritual warriors. She recalled their slaughter. Each person in that group was so unique and special. As a group, they could influence and manifest anything. Not many would have had the bravery to face a violent death as they had done. Each knew what was to pass, but also knew they had to die together in the formation of a circle, so they went to their deaths as they had lived their lives…together and as one.

Her eyes fluttered open; tears brimmed and began to overflow.

"Do not be sad, little one."

Adrienne turned to see Meha.

"Although in this lifetime you are no longer little. I still remember you very much as that brave child. Do not be sad about the circle."

Adrienne was quite surprised, wondering how he could have known her thoughts. He responded to her mental questions.

"It is one of my gifts, to read the thoughts as though they were words. Although, it does not always feel like a gift. Along with the thoughts, I will most times experience the emotion that accompanies the thought. I must be aware that if the person's sadness or anger is strong I must protect my own spirit. You should not feel sadness, you will be joined soon with the circle."

Meha looked out over the hillside. The fires burned so full and high that Adrienne could see his strong profile even in the darkness. His long, flowing hair was black as the night around them. The crystal on his cloak seemed to reflect the stars above. Adrienne felt a strong sense of security and safety while sitting with Meha. She had not felt this feeling of safety and strength in her recollection for many lifetimes.

They sat in silence for a while. She pondered the fear that she had lived with for so long, realizing now how profound that fearfulness had been in comparison to the feeling of strength of which she was now so keenly aware.

"Meha, how do you so easily recall our earlier lives?"

He was silent for a few minutes.

"The world is full of spirits that speak if you listen. I have always heard them speak. I learned if I spend time away and alone I would see as well as hear the stories to be told about the past. I have seen our fate in that lifetime."

"In wonderment, I pondered the cruelty of the dark one. I have spent a lifetime trying to understand the nature of what I originally thought was a cruel spirit."

Adrienne's eyes darted directly to his asking,

"What do you man 'originally thought?

What do you think is the meaning of what happened?"

Meha paused for a moment, and then responded.

"The beast for me reflects much of what you see as the worst of humankind, the mindless cruelty some inflict on others, murder, mayhem, behaviors intent on destruction. When you consider the violent crimes that are committed, every day, for seemingly no logical reason, it is staggering to the mind."

"These thoughts were in my mind during one of my spiritual quests. My guides showed me much about the history of these acts against humankind. Since the beginning of human existence on this planet, there has been a warring activity present. The battle is between the positive and negative of our species. At some point, we evolved into human form, then intellectual form, and then understandably, we multiplied. Different genetic codes, different body types, psychological, predispositions, every type of spiritual nature began to come into existence."

"Humans at some point became aware of the ability to manifest; to use some of their mental capacities to create. From this, we see an increase in what is frequently called good and evil, positive and negative, etc. Many people did not know they were creating; therefore, they attributed these activities to various gods, evil gods, heavenly gods, nature gods, etc. Many believed these gods brought justice, vengeance in fact, all that was prayed for, all that was asked for, but those prayers were the issuance of the human's manifestations of thought. The human consciousness was creating outcomes through the energy of their thoughts".

"As we gave power to these energies, a battle began. Now that humans numbered in the millions, the warring of the tribes and their cruelty and selfishness increased. Battling what they despised became more prevalent and many times the killing included many innocent people"

"People were murdered, beaten and tortured for dressing, speaking, thinking in any way that was deemed offensive. As the manifestation of cruelty became more pronounced, many groups formed in defense of these actions. Other groups just tried to 'live and let live' tried to live their lives without hurting or harming to anyone. Living independently, many other people chose not to be part of the more organized groups. Many others then called themselves religious, pious or devoted to some deity. Unfortunately, many of the organized religions became so fanatical in their beliefs and practices they began to be suspicious of, and sometimes persecute, anyone who was not fully accepting of their view. In some cases, the strength of this negativity assisted the energy manifestation of the existing mean-spirited people."

"What has happened over the history of humankind reflects the dynamics of the exchange of the energies. In fact, Adrienne, the spirit presence who wishes to destroy you is a being sustained by negative psychic energy. This energy source has been made strong by generations of evil thoughts and deeds. As the population of earth grew and there were followers of evildoers, so then did this presence gain energy and strength."

"The creature fights hard, knowing that the circle and all that it stands for would cause its demise. So, Adrienne, now you know, it's a struggle to the death. That is why the creature attacked the first circle, in the beginning. It was not aware of the full extent of your power. It did not understand the depth of your ability or the full concept of the circle. But many centuries have passed, and the creature has many generations of knowledge and has grown aware that you are a very serious threat."

Adrienne was completely overwhelmed with the complexity and totality of this flow of information. She sat still, knowing what Meha said was truth yet trying to deny the reality of his words.

Nasha walked toward them through the darkness, seeming to appear from nowhere. The fires had died down a bit. Seeing clearly in the smoky night air was very difficult. Adrienne could see that Nasha carried a basket which she sat on the ground between them. As she put a blanket down on the ground, she spoke.

"It is very late. Here is some food. You must eat and then you need sleep. I have prepared a place in a tee-pee below. Eat now, I will return with a torch to guide you down very soon."

Adrienne realized how hungry she was as the smell of the food wafted up from the basket when Meha removed the top. She and Meha ate in silence. Her thoughts were in a whirl. Yet, she still felt very strong and centered. As she sat with Meha, it was as though she was in the eye of the storm. As she pondered the concept, she realized her intuition was resonating accurately. In fact, they were all in the eye of the storm. Now, they had their temporary pause, knowing the second half, or second coming, if you prefer, would soon be upon them. She thought,

Humans have created this conflict, had they ever really known how high the stakes actually were?

Did they understand it would be such a critical battle; the testing of wills between positive and negative manifestations? It involved not some omnipotent, male god in the sky, but humanity, the circle, including herself, against a destructive energy force.

The circle was supported by centuries of commitment, there were many who manifested strength in the positive. There were many belief systems developed which sent only kindness into the universal consciousness. Adrienne pondered for a moment the countless thousands who, even now, were meditating across the planet. She thought about the Native American Indians who spoke of the birth of the white buffalo. This birth came as a sign that the spiritual balance of the world was shifting to the positive. These people gathered below in the valley seemed to have a very strong sense of this balance. Knowing this story about the American Indian perspective of this event, and the many cultures that had similar beliefs, helped to support her growing optimism.

Strangely, as this final conflict grew closer, Adrienne was gaining strength and hope. Her fear had actually diminished to some degree; her confidence steeled her determination to win this battle. Adrienne could see a torch making its way seemingly on its own toward them. She knew Nasha was returning to guide her and Meha back to the campgrounds.

"Meha, will we overcome this danger? You seem to have such knowledge about these events; can you know the future?"

He looked over the desert landscape, viewing what now totaled hundreds of tents, teepees, vans and RV's. Campfires burned very low as many were sleeping. The great expanse of land and mountains lay beyond. Meha could see the silhouettes of the huge mountainsides and knew the deep craters that lay in between. He had grown up in this area. Except for going away to college he had never left, never wished to go from this place. His answer was slow.

"Adrienne, I am tied to the land. That includes the spiritual aspects. Many of the spirits of my ancestors still remain. On occasion, the spirits have revealed a view of the future. This usually comes to me in a dream, or a mental vision of a part of the future. I do not yet have the whole picture, the complete view. I believe, from what I have seen, what has been revealed to me, is that you are chosen and we are the circle of souls destined to change the course of events for humankind. There are many people here below across the expanse of this valley and around the world who know of this final conflict. They know that we will reach the brink of this frightening event in less than one day. It is their strength, their positive focus on us, which is helping us to grow stronger each hour. Those combined energies will enable us to conquer this foe. This gives me the belief we will win the conflict. Meha paused and looked out across the expansive landscape. He spoke softly as he said,

"I have always gained much hope from the instruction of nature. When you ponder the fact that trees help clean our air; that the time and ways in which the earth turns allow for life to thrive in the proper temperatures; that the sun and rain in many parts of the world are in stable enough amounts to have supported life for many millions of years of recorded history, the intervention of humankind is what changes the balance. With humans, the strongest and the most adaptable, due to evolution or physical and spiritual selection, will survive and thrive for the benefit of the planet."

Nasha rounded the last corner. The torch gave off light that was initially harsh to Adrienne's eyes. When she blinked and her sight refocused, she saw Meha brush away a single tear that had fallen from his eyes. Adrienne marveled at life's dichotomies. Sitting with this powerful warrior, fierce as could be in battle, yet he carried with him equally pronounced empathy and emotional feeling for the sacred aspects of life. Nasha began to collect the basket and the blankets. Meha and Adrienne were silent as they began to prepare for the descent to the valley.

They walked in silence down the hill toward the camp. As they approached the base of the hill, an old woman approached Adrienne and took her hand.

"Follow me, I will guide you to your sleeping place."

Chapter Ninteen. The Vigil of

the Goddess...

As they approached the far side of the mountain, Adrienne saw a small bonfire with two women sitting beside the fire. They stood as Adrienne approached and each took one of her arms to guide her forward. As she walked ahead, she saw a large crevice in the side of the cave, which they then entered. A waterfall ran to the right of the crevice and formed a beautiful pool of water which reflected the light from the torches that the women carried. Adrienne felt as though she recalled this scene from another time. The older woman spoke to Adrienne and said.

"Tonight you will sleep with the mother. Enter her womb, rest and be safe from any harm. Dream, gather your strength and make ready for the battle which will come very soon."

They left Adrienne at the mouth of the cave to continue her journey alone, as was the tradition. They gave her a lantern so she could find her way to the final sleeping spot. As she walked along she began to look around and observe the sacred cave. The etchings on the walls, depicted stories of shape shifters, battles, birth, death, lust and hate. Sketches of things that women have seen, felt and recorded for future generations to view. This was a cave of guidance for women in passage. The cave has been used for generations to educate women in the ways of life. As Adrienne walked through the last cave slit, she saw the small, dark, round space, just large enough to curl her body into. A blanket had been placed inside and her lantern reflected enough so she could see her way to settle in for the night. Adrienne continued her introspection,

Recalling that the guides had spoken of this ritual which allows for no light unless one felt as though they needed it for an emergency egress of any kind. Tonight's ritual is to be practiced completely in the dark, in the womb of the earth, our mother, for comfort and protection. With the absence of light and any other personage, one can then connect alone with the essence of goddess energy.

Adrienne reflected again on her surroundings.

This space, the caves, reminded me so much of the memories from my regression work with Dr. Hart. In my past life experiences I had faced adversity and death on several occasions and survived. I thought I would be afraid, after everyone had departed the cave. Instead, I now feel complete calm and comfort. Perhaps my past life experiences have left me with more courage than I had realized possible.

Adrienne leaned her head against the side of a piece of rock. A rock that had been worn smooth by many other women in the past, she began to hear the quiet rush and gurgle of the waterfall. Adrienne was grateful for this place, and felt her eyes fluttering closed. As she blew out the flame of the lantern, only then did she realize how very tired she had become, sleep was welcome.

Chapter Twenty. Amenhotep...

Shanta could not help but wonder at the Fates, now listening to this cruel dictator. She missed her mother so much. She wondered why the new Pharaoh was in the position to be such a threat to her future, and thereby the future of the order. Shanta's thoughts focused on the other brother of the Pharaoh, the one she knew so well, her beloved, her betrothed. Even now as they were parted, they were joined. She, at sixteen, was soon to be wed, as arranged by her mother. Shanta's thoughts drifted to an afternoon not so long ago. The day was a most beautiful one, the skies a clear blue with only an occasional wisp of a white cloud. Shanta walked up the long wide steps leading to her wing of the palace. She stood at the side of the pool where the water was clear and still. She could see her image reflecting in the pool. Her handmaidens had worked very hard to braid her hair and weave gold and lapis beading at the end of each strand. On top of her head, a small crown of similar design and shading was delicately placed amidst her hair. Her slender body was fitted into a skirt of soft, white, silk- like material heavily embroidered with gold and lapis threads. She wore nothing else except her sandals and jewelry, all matched to similar shades. Shanta could not believe how grown up she now looked compared to just two years ago when she could not even walk properly in these tight, tapered skirts. All of her training in eye kohl, jewelry, and formal dress helped her to prepare for the first meetings with her betrothed. She thought she would be very nervous. She was surprised at how easy it was to be with him, even with so many others watching this historic event. She felt so at ease, and it would seem he felt the same about being with her. By age sixteen, she would be joined in ceremony with him, he, being only seventeen years old himself. While the upcoming ceremony was a formality where royal blood was joined for life, they had already consummated their love. From that time on, they spent as much time as they could together. Their intimacy, while difficult to arrange in such a public household, had inevitably been made possible by their friends, trusted handmaidens and servants.

Her thoughts returned from her reflection. Walking briskly to the archway, she opened the door and let her brother, the love of her life and soon to be her husband, into her chambers.

She looked upon his face. In her mind she always thought him beautiful even though that is not a word men use to describe their person. She nevertheless found him hypnotizing. Lost in his eyes, as he gazed upon her with complete adoration she had no doubts about loving him forever. They would be, as a matter of course, always bonded in their marriage commitment. She knew the law would allow for him eventually to have other wives. However, she would always be the principal wife: the first and most important. Also as his sister, would have a special place in his heart the others could not ever have. Amenhotep, while looking in her eyes, placed his hands on her hips.

"Shanta, I have missed you so."

She hugged him closely, feeling the warmth of his skin on her breasts. She loved the sensation. Moments they shared such as these she wished would never end. All of time seemed suspended. She forgot about everything else except their passion, loyalty and love for each other.

They sat in the corner in the shade of the palms. While eating some fruit, they spoke of the wedding, the gossip of their friends and family. It was still very warm, the sun descended in the sky and a slight breeze began to blow in from the balcony.

He looked at her, knowing he could love no other as he loved her. He teased her into taking off her dress and sandals and immersing herself in the reflecting pool. The water felt so cool. The pool was quite lovely and, while only a few feet in depth, very enjoyable for them on this hot evening. They climbed out of the pool and lay together staring up at the beautifully mosaic and painted high ceiling. They both agreed that this was a perfect moment and it must be what the afterlife is like. Much of how the afterlife was described seemed so ideal, they wondered why anyone would wish to return to an earthly existence. Together they agreed a divine existence for everyone would be penultimate. Then, they wondered if they would still be together. Even for the pleasure of an idyllic afterlife, they would never agree to be separated. Such was their bliss and depth of love. They agreed they were truly meant to be together for all eternity.

Shanta's thoughts drifted to the upcoming wedding ceremony. She became nervous at the thought of such a huge public service. Her last public ceremony was when she was chosen as the most revered goddess of the land, and her station in the royal family was acknowledged. She wondered if the circle would hold another private ceremony that would precede her nuptials, as they had done before her crowning ceremony. As with all important steps in her life, the secret ceremony would probably be observed. Her mind flew back to the room with the gilded statue beneath the hidden panels in the great hall. She recalled the time-worn statue. On its pedestal it seemed quite immense to her and, at the time, it seemed so very tall. Now, as she looked back, she realized the statue itself was probably not that tall and the base upon which the statue rested was what provided the illusion of impressive height. She realized, as she recalled the statue, there was no hair on its head, and, during the ceremony, a robe had been draped on the image. As she passed by it on previous occasions, she realized it was genderless, neither male nor female. Long, slender features, the most pronounced being the penetrating eyes, large and forgiving, almost seeking out the essence of each person who came to sit nearby and meditate.

A golden paste had been applied to the wooden statue for special occasions, one could observe the large cracks in what seemed to be very old ebony. The statue was neither male nor female. It was a sort of unisexual representation. No tokens were left, no sacrifices, just the offered intentions of the devotees. Generations had joined in adoration of this spiritual force. The focus of adoration allowed and encouraged thoughts of wisdom, compassion, and immersion within the power of positive thought. This supported the belief that anything a devotee aspired to could be achieved. As simple and as beautiful as the belief was, the group had always been forced to operate knowing that, if they were discovered, they would certainly be put to death by the more powerful religious orders.

Secrecy and devotion had been taught and practiced by countless generations of the circle. Established religions found the existence of this group particularly threatening. Too much freedom of spiritual choice was not welcomed in this era. Shanta's group had no written words, no obligatory financial donations, no control by threats or engendered guilt on any deed, as long as that deed did not harm another. The Circle possessed knowledge that life did continue if they chose to reincarnate, they did not have to have their organs removed as was the custom upon death. Nor were they forced to subscribe to current dogma of giving large sums of money and goods to high priests in order to live happily in the afterlife.

The fear the high priests had was, that if the secret circles spiritual practices were completely accepted into practice by the population at large, this belief system would dominate. This enlightenment would then eliminate the financial contributions used to subsidized priests who had great political power. The fear of their losing religious dominance along with its inherent revenue was why they killed her mother, and many others who had followed these peaceful practices.

Adrienne began to come to a higher level of consciousness and yet still in a trance light state thought:

Power. What did that really mean? In the hands of some, it had been used to distract humankind from their destiny, by focusing on the material instead of the spiritual. The control necessary to maintain mass dominance had become a perversion. However complex of a problem, I know in my heart that, as the Chosen, I can change this path. The day will come, as it has been told, that all of my spiritual family both seen and unseen will join, to alter the current course of events.

Chapter Twenty-one. Mandala of Hope...

Adrienne awakened in the dark with a start, and began to ponder the phrase she recalled.

"Alter the current course of the events."

In her consciousness, she began to recall the rest of the dream...

She focused on the sound of the waterfall. This had always been a favorite sound for her. It was comforting to hear the water. It reminded her that she was still connected to the present. Sleeping in this darkened cave was an experience that could be, at times, unsettling. However with no distractions, one tends to go to the most core aspects of one's thoughts.

She started to reflect on what she could recall of this dream. Adrienne realized that Shanta's thoughts and beliefs were integral to her in this lifetime. Perhaps that is why Adrienne was not inclined to be party to the more formal, organized religions. Many of the problems existing in her time as Shanta, still troubled Adrienne now. As a child in this lifetime Adrienne, had become suspiciously aware of organized belief systems. While her parents had her go through extensive religious training by the age of twelve, she had developed some doubts about the validity of the religion in which she suddenly found herself immersed. A religion that teaches messages of kindness and love while condoning holy wars seemed a contradiction to Adrienne. The duality of stated beliefs of love and truth, compared with how some people used religion as an excuse for cruel and selfish behavior, did not ring true to her thinking. Perhaps sleeping in the womb of the goddess cave did promote this focused spiritual awareness. It certainly had encouraged deep reflection in Adrienne.

Finally fully awake, Adrienne slowly began to uncurl from her resting spot and walked back toward the sound of the waterfall. When she reached the waterfall, she stood at the mouth of the cave, for a moment amazed at the beauty of this place. The sun had started to rise and splashes of sunshine refracted through the flowing waterfall. To her it seemed as though the reflections looked like pieces of gold with diamonds flowing in unison with the water. As she looked closer she could see etchings on the cave walls of women in various aspects of life, birthing, menstruating, defending their land and tribes as warriors and leaders. For many generations women had been painting their experiences. Documenting the past so the future generations could see what had transpired in their history.

Adrienne could see how some of the older sketches had faded and were reduced to a clay-like ochre color. As the techniques advanced, some of the drawings and the colors became more creative and more illustrative of the many life experiences depicted.

Adrienne stopped in front of one of the drawings she somehow knew well. Adrienne was shocked to see *the circle,* looking just like the one Dr. Hart had helped her identify in one of the regression sessions. This picture had a group of men and women in a circle- nine in all with a tenth person in the center. She then noticed a beautiful sand mandala. It was assumedly recent because the colors were so vivid, and therefore would have required extensive maintenance to keep up the colors as well as the design.

The mandala depicted a large circle. It was composed of a maze-like design of many concentric circles within circles, and yet upon staring at this for some time it appeared to her that all paths of the maze led to the same place, which was the center of the main circle. She assumed that to even design this intricate piece must have taken years of devotion and expertise to link all the mazes together. Adrienne marveled at this work and realized that there had to be a community of people living somewhere close by committed to the concepts of the circle. Apparently they had the same understanding as she now had that this mandala was intended as a guide for spiritual transformation. She drew comfort from the fact that there was such sustained commitment to this belief. Basically that people deserved and could create profound happiness. That was their gift from the spiritual source. Adrienne was equally in awe of the potential power all humanity had to bring death, famine, disease, cruelty and catastrophes of every kind. By believing in these things and, in most cases, wishing for them, they were created in this natural world by people of ill will.

So now, as Adrienne faced the final circle, she wondered were there enough people in this world that had purity and light in their hearts. Enough who could offset the negative powers that also existed? Had enough time passed, enough kind acts been demonstrated, enough speakers, writers and role models having acted in ways that nurtured the positive belief system? Her group had many adversaries. Those who spent many an hour in rituals devoted to murder, to mayhem, to the summoning and support of the essence of evil. As Adrienne continued to walk toward the mouth of the cave, she pondered.

In the end it comes down to how we as a people use mental energy. By using our thoughts we can create the best outcomes for our future, or the worst.

Adrienne reflected on the article that she had read several years ago about the prediction that, if the world were to survive, a white buffalo would be born around the time of the harmonic convergence. The American Indian tale stated this birth was a portent of the future of our world. If enough people worked toward the betterment of the planet and its' inhabitants then we would have a great chance of survival. As her mind searched for reasons she would be successful and survive in the final circle, she realized that she was forgetting to remain centered and grounded in her thoughts. Adrienne remembered that she had the power to change this course of events. She stepped into the center of the mandala to meditate, squatted down on her haunches, and closed her eyes, and began to envision her future. She pondered internally.

The future for me has to be about letting go of fear and believing in my success. Not giving power to my enemy, not even allowing my imagination to envision negative strength manifesting in any way. In effect, I have to create an altered state of reality for my psyche to exist within. This reality shows only me as the victor, being all powerful. While spiritually I understand this, my purely human side struggles with this belief. Therein lay my challenge: how to harness and control the drifting of my human doubts.

Adrienne could now see that elevating the human psyche up to a higher psycho spiritual level is difficult in this worldly plane, because the planet is now the center of conflict. The struggle between good and evil, is how the world has existed to date. The ebb and flow of these positive and negative emotions and then what we do about these emotions affect what happens in our world. The larger examples include wars. Smaller examples, include children intimidating the innocents of their peer group. Where does it begin, and how? These questions are pondered by many and learned from by few. Do the origins really matter? Yes, if we act with what is learned. So is it how and when we intervene to change the course of events? Did the world become paralyzed by long-winded analyses, on the root of evil, or by apathy such that we waited to long to stop these acts? Adrienne began to think to herself.

So, is it as simple as deciding what we stand for and then bringing that reality and consistency into our lives? To do that takes honesty and courage and the support of each other. I wondered if, in my case, the cruel creature who chases after me is an example of evil, once good and then gone astray. A "Teufelgeist", a ghost-demon. If that has truth to it, then if we work hard, over time the number of spirits in every negative dimension will diminish. Perhaps now there are so few of the demons left, they will grow lonely and die away. A beautiful thought, my hope for the future. But for now, it is up to me to begin to imagine the strength of my capabilities, the power of my spirit and the vision of my success.

As Adrienne opened her eyes she could see the most beautiful circle of fluttering butterflies, of many colors and sizes doing the most amazing dances. Theirs was a circular swirling dance of energy that was enough to transport her psyche to a place of wonder. Adrienne's eyes tried to follow one group that, even with their larger wings, were twirling in a close spiral around and around. She was amazed at how they could do this without touching or falling. How can I not be reminded of the miracles of nature and therefore the universe? Miracles abound with beauty; goodness has survived.

Adrienne arose to walk to the waterfall. Stepping under it, she imagined the flow of the water washing away all her doubts and restoring belief in her survival.

She stepped out of the water and looked up to see Asha approaching, with her beautiful eyes that, as Adrienne focused on them, seemed familiar to her. After this night of focused recollection, Adrienne was convinced that Asha was also Sosha, who helped her in the first circle. Those memories that had been recalled in the sessions with Dr. Hart were coming back. Adrienne felt so comforted by Asha's presence, as had been the case in the past. Asha watched Adrienne for a while, and then called out,

"Come, little one, the end of our journey grows near. Are you ready?"

Adrienne paused, and looked at Asha and stretched out her hand. Asha then held Adrienne's hand firmly and they began to walk to the sacred circle.

Chapter Twenty-two. Fate Brings the Circle Closer...

The bonfires were high and hot. Swarms of small fire flecks exploded like wild fireworks in the sky. The Indian tribes had gathered from many areas. The colors of the feathers and clothing were mesmerizing as people chanted and moved around the flames. Adrienne could feel the energy emitting from this gathering and it brought her strength. As she felt this strength, it brought peace and comfort. The group was at the last step of the journey; they would use the maps found in the village and on the tattoos to guide them to the sacred circle.

Adrienne's mind began to drift as she watched the ceremony. The day was passing by so fast, as though time was not operating by the usual standards, as though all of nature was rushing the ten to the circle. Adrienne recalled a story told earlier in the day. It was the tale of a village when all of the men, women and children forced to defend themselves against barbaric invaders. Knowing they could lose their lives in painful and violent fashion, they bonded together and, in their combined strength, they eventually survived. They discovered in this experience that they were all heroes, that each had courage deep in their hearts that was fueled by their love and compassion for each other and the tribe. Now, on the eve of this battle, Adrienne recalled the importance of this final conflict. The survival of the human tribe was at stake.

Suddenly, Adrienne heard horses galloping toward the camp. She could hear the hooves even over the sound of the drums, as they were galloping at a great speed. People from the village rode up and spoke of a message for her. An envelope was passed to Adrienne. She was surprised that a letter had been sent. What could this mean? She thought, as she opened the dusty envelope.

"Adrienne," She recognized her brother's handwriting immediately.

"I received your last letter and was concerned with some of the questions I had that you left unanswered. Then to add to the worry, I had a dream of frightening intensity. In the dream, I saw the face of a demon. Even with all of my religious training, I could not believe this vision. Even as I awoke from my dream, this beast-like apparition did not depart. Instead, it stayed for some long and fearful moments almost mocking or laughing at me. He told me to stay away from you, that you have angered him and that he would take your life if I helped you in any way. I was shocked with fear after he left, and realized this was the most dangerous spiritual conflict I could have imagined. I have taken leave from my parish assignment and am now en route to join you. I will be there in the morning. Do not depart without me. I now understand from my dream that I must be there to help you. Love, Mike"

Adrienne was shocked to think that the demon had made its presence know in Mike's life. It had shocked him to his core, and changed his life forever. She knew this had to be terrifying for him. His work had always involved helping the weak, the defenseless and the sick. This situation was so far from his daily reality Adrienne wondered about his emotional stability. She had always lived in a spiritual dichotomy, seeing things, people, visions others could not see-and then somehow finding ways to still work and thrive in day-to-day reality. However that had not been Mike's experience and she was very worried about him.

Adrienne would ask Dr. Hart to spend time with Mike after he arrived to help prepare him for what was happening with our group. Mike being the wonderful spirit he has been, needed to be saved for the world. Then Adrienne realized that, it is he and others like him everywhere that we seek to save and so it seemed this was all meant to be. She lay down in her teepee and thought back to the memory of the butterflies to help fall asleep.

The sun was just beginning to rise. Adrienne had never been one to be up with the dawn, but this day, after a night of unsettled sleep, she was awake. The teepee was quiet, with only the sounds of others breathing softly as they slept. She looked around the teepee top to see the drawings of the land. Nature, childbirth, and death - the drawings were simplistic yet profound in their message.

Life really is so simple in its rhythms. This thought brought Adrienne solace, as she wondered how she had arrived at this moment, at this place and with these people; that her life and many others around her had taken such a dramatic turn. Once, albeit with some psychological angst, Adrienne thought herself to be much like everyone else. Life was, at some points, almost mundane. Adrienne pondered,

To think that I had once made lists of weekend errands that included things such as a drive to the dry cleaners, or returning books to the library. How and when life had taken an abrupt turn and completely changed everything was still a source of wonderment. As I considered this question, I realized that, as my life had changed and members in my group's lives had changed, there were probably many other people all over the world who may be having partial recollections of past lives, or clues about their future work on this planet.

Adrienne thought about the future and how to connect with all of those people, she heard the sounds of hoof beats in the distance. They seemed to almost echo. She thought it her imagination at first and continued to listen. She began to hear birdcalls and whistles from the guards of the camp. They were signaling to the camp that visitors approached. Adrienne sat up and pulled off her covers, pulling on some clothes and grabbing a woolen cape to warm her from the chill of the morning. As she left the teepee, others began to stir. Adrienne walked out and splashed some water on her face. The water had gotten very cold in the night and felt like ice cubes against her skin. As she looked up, she could see a small group of riders approach the edge of the camp and tie up their horses. Adrienne knew they had to be friends or the guards would never have let them get this far into the camp. She stood and watched as the group approached. Adrienne could see faces now and recognized her brother among them. In regular travel clothes without his priest's collar, he looked so different; he seemed younger somehow and yet his expression was troubled. As the riders got down from their horses, Adrienne waved to welcome him. Mike's stride was swift as he approached and gave her a hug. He stood back and looked at her for a moment, and then said.

"Adrienne, why did you wait so long to write? I have been so worried about you I was determined to track you down. I could not get any answer at home and finally called Dr. Hart's office to see if I could get any information and was surprised to find you, and he, and some others were here."

He paused, almost tearful, and said,

"Adrienne, what is happening here?"

"Oh, Mike, where to begin? The past life regression work I have been doing with Dr. Hart along with the research that has been done has revealed a great deal more than I ever thought possible. In essence, what is happening here is a standoff, a final closing of a sacred circle that began with the origins of spirituality."

Adrienne explained that she was very central to this whole group.

"I had hoped you would be spared all of this, but apparently you are meant to be a part of this work this group is now doing together. Since the group leaves today for the last part of our journey to the original site of the circle, you should join us."

Adrienne explained that she was there in the beginning and must now take her place again.

Mike looked as though he could not speak, and his eyes stared deeply into Adrienne's.

"Adrienne, why do you believe this to be true? How has all of this come to pass?"

"I knew this would be very hard for you, Mike. Dr. Hart has a lot of the transcripts and tapes with him which track the initial regression and then the trip to Egypt to validate one of the past lives. I think if you can review our research, it will help you to understand the background of why we are here today. I know this departs from some of the experiences you've had and beliefs you have been taught, but hear Dr. Hart out and then we can talk more about it. Time grows so short, and we must continue our journey, which begins in a couple of hours. We have set up a place for you to get some sleep and have something to eat before we travel again. While I would love to just walk and talk more with you, I'm worried that you will not be strong and rested for our journey and our circle. We all must do the best we can to stay strong physically and emotionally."

Adrienne hugged her brother, wishing him protection from harm.

"Love you, Mike. Thank you so much for coming."

"Oh yeah, as if I would have postponed this for any reason. While it's a far cry from the work I was doing, I would not have you go through this without me."

Adrienne felt as though another piece of her "clicked" together, that somehow Mike's being here was helping her become stronger. Maybe he felt that way a little bit also. His face had a slight smile on it as he walked toward his teepee.

Back in Adrienne's teepee, as everyone sat on the ground looking over Dr. Hart's information. Asha's hand was around Adrienne's shoulder. She was supporting her back in such a protective way. Adrienne, Dr. Hart and Asha poured over the details of the photographs that Dr. Hart had taken at the cave when the two women were killed. There were also photos from the ceiling in the old church in the valley and the pictures of the women's tattoos. They continued to put together the pieces of what was essentially becoming a map. Asha spoke first.

"I can see it clearly now. I have walked these lands my entire life. The path leads us to a valley that is very close to where we are. We can reach this place in a few hours."

She stared intently at the drawing she was now sketching. She seemed to be guided intuitively by these fractured clues left for many hundred of years by people passing this wisdom down through generations of families. As she looked up into Adrienne's eyes, for a moment her face seemed to slightly alter its features. Still an older woman, her eyes seemed so blue and her hair seemed to be whiter and fuller around her face. At first, Adrienne was startled and somewhat frightened. She simultaneously realized that the face seemed almost identical to the description of the one Dr. Hart and she had culled from the video and audio tapes of her past life regression. This person was somehow spiritually still Shosha, Adrienne's guide and teacher when she lived as Rina. At first, Adrienne did not want to articulate this thought, but then realized, who better to discuss this belief with?

"Dr. Hart, could we talk with Asha about the work you did with me in past-life regression? Could you explain what we did, what the process was and what we discovered about my life as Rina?"

Dr. Hart looked at me quizzically, saying,

"We could, but with so little time left, would that help us now?"

"I feel as though Asha and I have a strong connection and I would like her to understand how regressions works, and that, as I have discovered, I lived before and who I was. She could do the same. Asha, if you are willing, I would like Dr. Hart to see if we had a connection before this life. He could do one session with you if you would trust us to do this work with you. Please, Dr. Hart, just explain how you do this work."

Asha smiled, her face crinkling up in a joyful way.

"Adrienne, I feel the connection that you speak of. We do not need another person to tell us of that."

Adrienne realized Asha's sense of this connection had been as strong as hers had been. Then a second flash came to her mind. Just as we were able to gain valuable information about life as Rina, we could gain insight about Asha's life as Shosha. Adrienne explained the thought to Dr. Hart and Asha. Asha seemed hesitant.

"Asha, I would ask that we do this together. I will sit with you, but because I believe we were in the circle together in the beginning and will soon be again, it would help me to hear whatever Dr. Hart can discover."

Adrienne put her hand around Asha's back and shoulders for comfort. Asha finally looked into Adrienne's eyes. Slowly Asha nodded and said,

"We shall do this."

Dr. Hart prepared a space in a teepee set up at the far end of the camp.

We sat in the darkened interior. Adrienne's observations drifted, and she began to think to herself. She sat looking at the symbols on the interior of the teepee, symbols of nature, the sun and moon, as she thought.

These have always been mystical favorites of mine in this life. Now I know more about why that had been the case, realizing I had been schooled in past lives with the observations and celebrations of the rituals of the sun god in as Shanta and with the moon goddess as Rina. These were feelings that came from my practices as a central figure in rituals from centuries long passed. Life is full of magic and miracles, some still unknown or unseen by many, but present nevertheless.

Dr. Hart began the hypnotic regression with Asha. He proceeded slowly allowing her to relax and count back in time and through space to allow her past to surface. He was asking her to go back into and through many lives until he helped her to find her life when she was teacher, spiritual advisor and guide to a young girl, named Rina. Dr. Hart guided Asha to the last day of her life as Shosha.

"Describe what is happening in the valley at the entrance to the sacred cave.

"The circle is to form."

Dr. Hart was directing her in this way to bring Asha closer to this event.

"We are coming together. I am holding Rina's hand. I know from the prophecy we will not survive this day. Rina is the most important of all. I must help her leave her body before the cursed one arrives. He would seek to destroy her spirit to banish her from his future. He would also, use her tortured body to frighten the sacred ones for all time. I know his dark thoughts too well. My psychic abilities are so strong I have long been aware of his evil plans.

He is the epitome of cruelty; he has no sense of right or wrong. He only seeks to win. He cannot access my thoughts, however, although he has attempted many times. I am too strong. That is why I have Rina live in the sacred cave with me. There is too much power in the cave from all the Ceremonies and I have trained her and protected her daily. It has been sad for me to know that she will not survive to adulthood and take her full power and place in the circle. But I know we will return. She is the center and the key, so it is spoken, so it shall be."

She paused for a few moments, and then began to speak again.

"We are together now. I see the evil plague in his human form. He is dressed in clothing to give the appearance that he is a demon. He wishes to frighten all who look upon him. There are very few living who know the truth that his true spirit is why the word *demon* was created.

"I look at his hateful face, and again I glance at my Rina. It is a strong temptation for me to use the incantations to destroy him."

Dr. Hart looked at me for a moment, paused and then asked,

"Asha, tell me of these incantations."

"They come from the mother. They have all the power needed to shift events as needed."

Dr. Hart asked, "How did you learn of these incantations?"

Asha replied, "My teacher showed me the symbols and taught me the chants."

"So it's both chanting and the use of sacred symbols that can be used to change events?"

"Yes, this is true," Asha began, "but should not be used to change the prophecy."

Dr. Hart inquired, "So your tribe and teacher had prophesied on what was to happen this day and you felt you should not use your power to change what was to happen?"

Asha responded, "Yes, that is so."

"Can you speak the chant, just the words, not the intent, so I may hear?"

Adrienne could hardly breathe as she realized what was happening. All was quiet, as Asha chanted. It was a beautiful sound, Adrienne was glad Dr. Hart was taping this session, so she could listen to this chant again. In the distance, she could hear a herd of horses, a powerful sound. She could not help for a minute to think about how many people were present to support this circle; thousands more than the first time, they had been together for such a conflict.

As Asha finished her singing Dr. Hart said,

"Is the chant sung by just one to change the course of events?"

Asha said, "Sung by one, or more –the outcome is the same. But taught to two in case the first falls in death."

Dr. Hart asked,

"And the symbols? Also taught to two?"

"Yes, the symbols are taught to two. I taught Rina, but she was still young and new in the practice of her power. She did not realize her strength."

"Asha, can you write the symbols for me?"

"They are not for anyone but The Chosen to see. I have them in the cave where she studies."

"The cave?"

Asha paused, then said.

"Yes, the sacred cave in the valley. They are etched in stone as was given to me. I hid the stone deep in the chamber when the evil one was coming, so I could protect the power."

Dr. Hart paused, then asked Asha,

"Where did you put the stone with the carvings?"

"Where the water begins, under the sacred chamber altar stone. The circle is upon it. I am glad I put it in so far from my reach, for when I saw the evil one, I was tempted to run and get it to go against prophesy and save my little one, Rina. It was hard to hold off cursing him. I know her future destiny was critical to the world, but I had anger in my heart for what was to happen; her death, the violence upon her body, brought a clash of my feelings so strong I could barely control them. But as I looked at her face, trusting in me, he was already riding toward us. I knew then I had to save her spirit; begin the ascension of our souls. We had to escape to our astral level to preserve her from harm and fear.

She was full of courage in the face of her fear. I was proud, and deeply sad at the same time. And so it was I who held her hand and we began to show our spirits the path of escape. Our bodies remained; his fury was unleashed by hacking up the physical remains, but he knew enough to understand that our spirits had left our bodies. He vowed revenge and screamed that he would have her, have victory. As we went into the astral plane, I knew he would not win. I know the prophecy."

"It will be he who dies. Humankind will grow in numbers and time will show what comes of his cruel beliefs and with him only pain and misery will abound. The knowledge and constant demonstration of kindness is the only thing that will shift the balance. It is the balance of positive beliefs that will cause his demise, and end his following. Rina will be in the circle as the keeper of the knowledge. I die knowing this and take comfort that she and I will return together."

Dr. Hart sat alone and, despite all of his experience, realized that this journey and these events were so far from any work he had done in the past. He could not help but be intimidated by the collection of information he and his team had compiled. He realized that Asha's regression had revealed what appeared to be a crucial missing key to the survival of this band of people, probably including his own life as well, given what he now knew of this circle. He slowly brought Asha out of her hypnotic state.

He realized the time was near to forming of the final circle. He needed to get some help to use his laptop to transcribe and print out the sounds and words of the chant so copies could be printed for everyone to use. These were ancient, powerful words that had been kept secret until today and he could not help but respect the synchronicity to these events.

This comes at a time to save us all.

Even as he thought about this, he still realized he was afraid, and as he pondered this, he thought, *why not?* This is the most formidable opponent any of us would ever face in this lifetime. Despite his fear, he was ever the man of science, still thinking logically. He needed Ona and Hans as soon as possible. Also, he wondered about the batteries on the laptop computers.

Would they last long enough for us to get this information printed out so the entire group could see these words and be able to help with the chant?

In addition, how to find the buried symbols in the cave. His anxiety about the rush to get these things accomplished prompted him to get up and move immediately. Adrienne said she would stay with Asha. Nodding, Dr. Hart picked up the tapes and computer and walked out of the teepee to search for Ona and Hans.

Adrienne sat alone with Asha holding her hand and allowing her time to think through the regression and the information that had been revealed.

Asha spoke,

"I was your teacher. Now you are mine."

Adrienne smiled at this old tribal sage and hugged her saying,

"Asha, I am not your teacher. You were mine many centuries ago, many lifetimes ago. We have both learned more about ourselves, the world, and what we must do.

I am not superior or teacher to you. We are partners in our spiritual strength. I very much need you, as you now need me. So we share our energy and knowledge as well as our love and respect for each other. They are the qualities that will make us strong and we will need this strength as we face what I have come to call 'The Teufelgeist, *the ghost demon'*. He is the collective energy given to him by many who seek power in this existence by using the dark, negative energies to accomplish the cruelty that they thrive on."

Adrienne continued,

"The circle will break that cycle of cruelty. Without that change, the world as we know it would end. What would remain would be worse than what has been depicted in writing regarding the Christian interpretation of hell, being forced for eternity to suffer constantly. That is what our fate is unless we stop it in the circle."

Asha and Adrienne sat together until the sound of horse's hooves could be heard approaching the teepee.

Adrienne could see Mike walking towards her from a distance. She could see his dark hair blowing in the breeze. As he grew closer, she had a vision and his appearance changed somehow. She thought at first that her eyes must have had dust blown into them, she closed her eyes for a moment and blinked. As she opened her eyes and looked again, he looked similar in his basic facial features, but he had a long beard and was dressed in a loose-flowing garment. He looked somewhat thinner in the loose tunic with smock-like inner robe, tied only with what looked like a coarse rope around his waist. He had a tall staff that he leaned upon to balance out the terrain as he walked. He had a peaceful look on his face. As the wind blew, it pushed back the cloak he wore over his tunic. The hood of his cloak shifted a bit to the side to show longer hair that was tucked under the hood. He looked like a man who was without means, very humble in his dress and demeanor. As he waved,

I wondered, is this man waving at me?

Adrienne thought it was Mike, but now she could see from his clothing this had to be someone else, someone who knew her.

The wind shifted again, dust beginning to swirl around. Adrienne closed her eyes to clear them, and as she opened them again, Mike looked to be his usual self again. Adrienne was unable to speak as he sat beside her.

"Adrienne, you look as though you have seen a ghost."

Adrienne stared at Michael, now seeing him as he usually looked. For a moment she wondered if she should speak at all of this occurrence. Surely, he might think her delusional. Adrienne recalled how close they had been before he went into the priesthood. Surely people can't change so much from their original belief system.

When they were children in their current lives, they had some experiences that were pretty amazing as she recalled. Adrienne thought about the time she decided to play hide and seek and found a wonderful place to hide was outside a window on the seventh floor of a high-rise building they were visiting. Well, of course it was definitely a place no one could find her, and she was so pleased about that. However, soon her slender fingers began to slip slowly from the concrete window ledge. Adrienne began to realize she would eventually drop and fall down from this great height to the concrete below. Even as a small child, she knew she could not survive such a fall. So, her weak voice, called shakily for her brother who, somehow heard…even though the apartment was quite large. He came to her rescue just as the small, sweaty fingers were slipping off the end of the ledge. Suddenly, she felt a strong hand at the top of her dress. Her younger brother seemed to have amazing strength for his age. He was still very small, and Adrienne was older and taller, but he grabbed the back of her dress and pulled her up in two quick tugs. Adrienne's recalled, he saved her life when no one else could have done so. As she recalled this incident, all these years later, remembering the fear she had when she realized she was slipping and would not survive such a fall.

Suddenly, Adrienne had a psychic flashback to an ancient time in history when, Michael was traveler who spent his life helping people. Her memory brought back a scene in time when

Michael had the same appearance and clothing that Adrienne had just seen him in a few moments ago, a loose tunic and cloak. He was leaning over a body on the side of a forested path. He was pushing back the matted hair of a woman who, at first, appeared dead. He covered her with his cloak; even though it was cold he took off his only protection against the elements to help this woman. He reached for his small leather pouch and held the liquid contents to the woman's mouth. He patted her forehead, tucking the cloak around her. He quickly began to build a small fire to warm this helpless woman. His face was clearly troubled and showed his worry about her condition. She was, as far as Adrienne could see, in a wretched state. She was filthy, her lips cracked and now slightly bleeding from moving them to try to drink the fluid. Her face was dirty, caked in some spots with mud. Her clothing was ripped and worn to not much more than rags. As he tried to put his blanket roll under her head, he straightened her neck and pulled her arm from the twisted position it had been in under her body. She groaned slightly and as he moved her very gently, it was clear she had been lying there for several days. Adrienne saw a sudden look of shock on his face as he noticed an intricate tattoo design on her wrist. He stopped and just stared in disbelief as he studied this design. As he looked closely at her arm, the inscription clearly meant something significant to him. Adrienne could now, see the woman's face much more closely and mentally realized with shock *this woman was my look-alike in her facial features, which however distorted in pain, showed a clear mirror image of my face although the hair was red and the eyes looked almost green. However strange the vision, this was definitely Michael and he was saving my life again in another time.*

Adrienne watched as he looked again at the tattoo design. He looked even more worried, almost fearful now. He looked around, spotting a small cave-like structure farther back in the woods. He quickly put the small fire out and put dirt and stones over the site where the fire had been. He gently picked up the woman and carried her to the cave. He went inside in the back section of the cave, taking the woman out of view, and put her down. He came back quickly for his staff, blanket roll and the leather pouch and then disappeared from view.

"Adrienne! Adrienne!" I could feel my arm being tugged. Michael was sitting beside me. "Are you okay? I was talking to you and realized you did not seem to be able to hear me. What's wrong?"

"Mike, I was truly a million miles in time and space from here." I began to tell him what had happened. His facial expression was very open, but I could tell he was as surprised as I was about all this.

"Mike, all I can say is that the universal Source has chosen to help me understand we have a bond that goes much further back than this lifetime. That you had at least one other lifetime when we met and you had intervened to try to save me from dying."

Mike sat and looked away for a few minutes. Finally he looked up and said,

"Well, I felt drawn to be here and that I needed to be by your side. So, some of these things seem to make sense in that regard. But, I need to think through some of the rest of what you have just told me."

"Mike, I must begin to travel this morning, but you could leave with the group who are working on making copies of the chart."

Mike nodded and finally said,

"Well, my decision to take a leave from the priesthood was a big one and part of that choice was so that I can live my life in a broader way. To expand how I am living in my spiritual view. Perhaps all of these things unfolding are part of this journey. To be open to finding out how I fit and can make a meaningful contribution in this world."

Adrienne said,

"Let's go to Dr. Hart's tent so you and he can discuss what has happened. Then I must go get Asha and the others. Our guide has already rounded up the horses," Adrienne spoke as she walked. They arrived at Dr. Hart's tent and briefly explained this surprise event of Adrienne's being able to see back into another lifetime without having Dr. Hart present in a waking session. Asha walked in as they finished the explanation of what had occurred. She nodded knowingly.

"Adrienne, do not be surprised. This gift is just one of the many that you have but have not really used in this lifetime. Now that you grow closer to the sacred circle and the land where your ancestors spent many hundreds of years, blessing the land with incantations of power and protection, you are starting to feel this power of yours. You will find many other things may start occurring so do not be startled. I can help you as you experience these flashes of insight; if you need to talk you can find me or when you are ready just speak it to me in your mind. I will hear and respond."

"Telepathic communication?" Dr. Hart inquired.

Asha nodded, and said "If that is your word for speaking through minds then, yes, it is so."

The guide arrived at the tent door. He announced,

"We are ready to go. Do you have your things?"

Adrienne and Asha nodded their heads in affirmation that they had their things, but as for feeling ready, Adrienne still felt concern tug at her. She hugged Mike and Dr. Hart and they compared maps once more and agreed on an exact time and place to meet. Dr. Hart was going to get Hans, Ona, Gina and Santee together.

Before Adrienne knew it, they were waving goodbye to a camp almost completely disassembled and repacked on horses and wagons. Vans and trailers of the scientific team were on the farthest part of the encampment and people were running in and out with an obvious need to finish up the remaining work and move out toward the desert road to their final destination.

Adrienne rode on her horse looking straight ahead and marveling at the beautiful skyline. It was peach and pink and light blue with streams of yellow with an almost golden-like shimmer to the color. She was lost in the splendor of yet another one of the universe's miracles. The beauty of this wonder filled her heart with hope and courage and somehow she was feeling all was as it should be and she was on the right path. She pondered all of the events that had occurred as she approached this final circle, realizing in a flash of insight that her life journey had been a series of miracles. There were many things that she had grown accustomed to but, in fact, were quite remarkable and very different from most people's lives. She wondered at the paths that people's lives can take, wondered at how she could be so different and why her life was the one chosen to journey on the lonely road of uncertainty. Yet, the miracles that she had seen along her path were so profound that she thought she must be spiritually supported and protected in many ways or she would not have gotten this far.

Also, to have found so many wonderful guides and helpers in this lifetime and to have been able to connect with some of her closest allies from another time was absolutely amazing to her.

"I am truly blessed," she spoke aloud in a whisper to herself.

Incredibly Asha, riding behind her, nodded and responded,

"It is so."

Asha pulled her horse up closer to Adrienne and, riding alongside her, said,

"I have something very special for you to wear in the circle. It has been made by the hands of many who travel with us now and will provide a psychic shield. It was made with love for a leader we cherish.

"Adrienne's eyes filled with tears. She was speechless for a moment and when she tried to speak, realized all she could manage to say was an emotional sounding,

"Thank you."

Adrienne was so touched by this very special gift, she was speechless. Asha seemed to understand her feelings and allowed her the time to be alone with her thoughts.

Feeling so connected to this group and the tribes that had gathered with her, Adrienne felt so complete. She felt more relaxed and happy when she was part of this spiritually connected family. The comparison of how she felt with them and how she had lived her life up until now was dramatic in her mind.

This security she felt allowed her to experience a depth of acceptance and belonging that had seemed lacking to some degree in her current life. The more she considered the concept for herself, she thought there were probably others who felt that way as well. She could imagine herself moving to this part of the world and spending time on a spiritual journey, one very different from the current journey that had been filled with trepidation. Adrienne was learning that we can be stronger than our fears but only if we genuinely affirm that to be the case. So, there are no lies in the spiritual realm, the truth of our thinking is our guide.

She pondered part of an old phrase she could barely recall, something about being "captain of your own ship, master of your own fate." The sentiment resonated so true and yet seemed simplistic in the basic phraseology. Living the reality was another matter. Spiritually we must have full belief that our "ship", if you will, is going safely to the destination we envision. Our thinking about and affirming of success or failure is key. Wavering from our destination, either due to fear or distraction can take us off course to a place or experience we did not desire. And yet, how many people really are cognizant of this fact? How many believe its other people or events that dictate their life's direction, therefore, giving up their ability to manifest their own personal miracles.

Asha rode up beside her, saying,

"We will camp soon to rest the horses and eat something. We will be stopping up ahead, to a campsite well known to the tribe."

Adrienne nodded as and pulled the reins slightly to the right and left to keep the horse on the more traveled pathway. The dust was billowing up and swirling around her face. She saw Asha pull up her shirt to cover her nose and mouth. Adrienne did the same, and it helped her breathing, but seeing was still difficult. As she rode along, she began to scan the mountainside. It was amazing how flat the land had been and now we were close to a steep slope of a mountain.

Adrienne stared up at the mountain and squinted as the sun shone directly into her eyes.

She thought for a moment that she saw a man on horseback at the top of the ridge. It was the silhouette of a man, but feathers seemed to flutter around the man's body. Adrienne blinked her eyes, thinking this would clear her view. When she looked again, there was no one there. She kept looking again at the same place, and then scanned the horizon but saw nothing. Adrienne turned to look at Asha to see if perhaps she had seen something. As Adrienne turned, Asha's eyes were warning her - Asha shook her head, as if to say, "No, don't speak now."

Somehow, Adrienne knew Asha meant for us to talk about this when we were away from the others. So, Adrienne turned back and just kept checking every so often to see if the mystery visitor would reappear. After seeing nothing for the next twenty minutes or so, she stopped looking. By then, we had reached the top of a small incline and Adrienne looked down to see a beautiful scene, a large pond with some shade and some of the tribe already setting up camp. Suddenly, she realized that she was tired, dusty and sore from riding, so the view of the water and the food cooking was a very welcome sight. It was agreed by the group we should have siesta here. Temporary tents were set up so people could rest in the shaded areas after lunch. While she was anxious to get to the final circle, the heat was intense, resting now made sense. Sitting inside the tent with the flaps on the side open gave shelter from the sun and allowed a slight breeze to float in from the pond, Adrienne began to feel a bit cooler.

The food was being set out on tables and everyone was starting to gather around to get something to eat and drink. We had not stopped since early morning and we were all really hungry.

As Adrienne sat down and began to eat, she was surprised to discover that she could not finish her plate of food. Between the heat and being nervous about the final circle coming together, and what that could mean, she couldn't eat. Adrienne did at least manage to drink a little more. As she put down her mug, Asha appeared.

"I have something for you and we must talk" she stated.

Adrienne looked at her wizened face, but only focused on her eyes. They seemed so knowing. Somehow looking into those eyes and having Asha there with her, made her feel more relaxed.

Adrienne and Asha walked slowly through the heat toward the edge of the pond and wooded area. As they traveled through the trees with their protective shade, Adrienne's eyes adjusted to the more darkened area of land. Adrienne was surprised to see a cave in between two huge boulders. Asha led her through the walkway between the boulders and they entered a cave, one with no light inside at all. Adrienne stood in the dark as Asha lit a torch. At once, light flooded the chamber. Adrienne could see a blanket and some items spread across some of the stones inside the cave. She looked at Asha, and she said to Adrienne.

"Come, these are for you. Let me explain the meaning of these things."

Adrienne could hear water trickling somewhere in the back of this cave. Asha explained this was considered an ancient and sacred spot by the spiritual community.

"Many generations have come here for special ceremonies. In the early days, it was always foretold that a leader would come and lead the tribes to a better life. Life with a greater happiness and high value on equality for everyone. With that as a foundation for all people, goodness and light surrounded all human, animal and plant life again, as it once had been in the origin of time."

Asha explained that, in preparation for this leader, a beautiful cloak had been made and tended to each year. She went to the side of the cave and pulled away a wooden door covered with

243

twigs and brush. Inside was a box covered on the outside with shells and crystal with lapis lazuli stones in beautiful circles and shapes. The box was lined with cedar wood, sanded down smoothly and then a large woven blanket. Asha opened the blanket and the most amazing cloak of feathers was inside. This cloak was also accompanied by a headdress of feathers.

"Adrienne, you are the person that was born to wear this. Please rise and let me put this cape on your shoulders."

As she pulled out the cloak, Adrienne looked and recalled her dream which she thought was a past life experience, and now she saw it was in her future time.

"Asha, I saw this in a dream, but also there were three animals with me - a white snowy owl on my shoulder, and two white wolves one on each side of me."

Asha nodded saying, "You have great wisdom as shown by the owl and you are surrounded by strength as shown by the wolves."

She attached the feathered headpiece, which had a band of beautiful beading and crystals. Hanging from either side were small clusters of white and blue feathers. The cloak was amazing;

the weaving and intricacy of the feathers were like a beautiful expression of the perfection that nature can create when in harmony. The arms of this cloak allowed for stretching the arms out so that, from the back, the body appeared to be a bird in flight. The feathers were predominantly white, with the neckline area done in multicolored feathers.

Asha explained this cloak was made for the soaring spirit to take flight; to rise to higher planes of consciousness.

"Adrienne, you will need this for the circle. The history of this cape comes from an earlier time, which is why the horseman you saw at the top of the mountain wore feathers. He is dressed as he once was when you and I saw him many generations ago in the original circle."

"Asha, so it was him again?"

Asha heard Adrienne's voice rise in concern, she could not help but express her fear at his continued presence.

"Yes, it was him. But, Adrienne, remember well, he is not the enemy. That is illusion. The only real enemy is your fear. Your belief about his strength, or lack of it, will dictate the outcome. Be strong, and know that it is foretold you will emerge as leader. But the key to that prediction is that your strength and belief in yourself remain unwavering. I will leave you here for a while as the others sleep. You can connect with your spirit guides and power animals. Fortify yourself and then we will join forces to defeat the evil one."

As Adrienne sat to meditate and calm herself, she felt the tension in her shoulders. The stress of these events was clearly evident in her stiff body. She thought:

You can try and trick the mind, but the body refuses to lie to you.

Adrienne knew if she focused, she could center herself. She knew that she must get more settled, more grounded. Adrienne would use the mental exercise she learned when she took her meditation class. That usually worked. So she took a breath and began: up the stairs, through the doors, to the garden she now knew so well. It was beautiful there. She mentally walked down the path, past the trees that grew in such lush abundance. She felt so peaceful here; the grass felt soft under her bare feet. Adrienne loved the feeling of being so free, so safe and content. She continued walking to the lakeside and rested in the hammock that hung from two trees. The lake was very large, however the small island in the center was within easy view. Adrienne stared at the water; the shimmers looked to her like little diamonds sprinkled across the tips of subtle ripples in the water. She was happy here in this place. It was a place in space and time that she had created just for herself.

All the cares of the world were nonexistent here; no sorrow, no illness, no fear. What a beautiful paradise, a center of hope within her spirit. Yet, it took her years to know of this calm within herself. This is the essence of the goddess within. There is sacred space within everyone, but how many people cultivate that space for themselves? She wondered. How many even knew they could create such a miracle? So, this would be a Garden of Eden that some say was taken away by doubting the sacred word of God. Perhaps the only thing separating humankind from this original gift was just the veil of doubt. If you go to the gardens in your mind and spirit, all the beauty of the divine is present.

As Adrienne pondered this in her mediation, it became clear that this concept was a universal truth, known to many and yet unknown to the majority of our cultures. This would be another challenge going forward. Many more would need to connect to their inner spirituality so that our universe could glow with higher degrees of love and trust, creating more safety and security in our lives. This would be part of the work of the circle, to help people see the incredible options available to them as individuals and to our world community.

Adrienne knew it was time to go back, and slowly mentally she began her steps to return. She felt very happy, relaxed and strengthened in her resolve. Her reconnecting with the universal Source had, once again, provided a priceless gift.

Adrienne came back to the sounds of the present, birds singing, the wind slightly shifting the leaves, and the natural world seemed a beautiful place. She loved so many things about being in nature, which provided her even more resolve to do all that she could to protect our natural home.

She stood and began walking toward Asha.

"We should leave," Adrienne said. Asha nodded and they headed for our horses. The last leg of our journey had begun.

The trail was hot and dusty, and many times Adrienne longed to stop and find a place with shade and a cool drink. However, they were both aware that time was precious and so they pressed on determinedly toward their destination. Just as they reached the peak of one long and dusty hill, they saw the encampment at last. It seemed as though there were many more people than had gathered at the last campsite. The increase in support cheered Adrienne, although the actual inner circle could never be more than ten people, knowing that there were so many supporting them was a good feeling.

As they came close to the camp Adrienne could see Dr. Hart and Hans waving. He was smiling, so she took that as a good sign. Adrienne was hoping that he had been able to pull together all the resources needed to interpret the chant and the symbols they would need. They tied up their horses, and Asha gently removed Adrienne's cloak and headdress from her backpack. Hans gave Adrienne a hug as Dr. Hart looked at the garments with appreciation. Asha saw Dr. Hart looking at the robes. He walked closer to them to get a better view.

"What are these?"

Dr. Hart inquired. Asha was deep in explanation of the symbolism and the meaning of the garments and how they fit into the plans for the final circle. Adrienne was suddenly distracted by the sounds in the distance. She immediately began walking toward the sound of the singing and chanting. As Adrienne walked closer she could hear an underlying rhythm of drums. She felt so much at home as she sat and listened. Adrienne felt as though she belonged here more than anywhere on earth. That seemed odd to her, as she had just arrived in this place. Adrienne was aware of Asha standing behind her, and then putting a hand on her shoulder. Adrienne wondered about all she had read in Carl Jung's work regarding genetic memory. She now felt that she was a walking example of this theory, as she listened to the chanting of these people getting ready for the final circle.

They practiced the words that Dr. Hart had transcribed and provided to everyone so that they could sing these words together. Synchronicity is amazing. It is one thing to hear about these examples and quite another to experience them firsthand. Adrienne stood for a moment in awe of the sounds and feelings the chanting generated in her, and she wondered if others were as emotionally touched by the sounds as she was.

Chapter Twenty-three. Final Conflict...

It was now Twilight. Everyone began to move faster as the sun set. The temperature was cooler now, so people could hasten to complete their work. Asha directed the final preparation of the ceremony site where the inner circle was located. She had found the ancient symbols from the cave where they had been hidden for so long. She etched them around the circle. The other intricate sand designs had been completed before they had arrived. The colors and designs looked like a language from another time and place, a time when the universe was infused with spirituality and many more people supported the divine practices. There was more time devoted to healing and taking care of people, animals and nature in general in a more considerate way. Time was not spent at war. Disagreements were settled through dialogue and mutual respect in order to maintain the balance of the earth and all the creatures that lived on the planet. Somehow there was also an inherent knowledge that the balance of the earth had a symbiotic relationship with the balance of the universe.

Tonight there would be a full moon, and as the moon began to rise it was taking on a deep orange hue, which made it seem so close, as though it were trying to provide the light for the ceremony. As the time grew closer, Adrienne was led off to a teepee to wash and change for the ritual. Some fruit and water had been left for her as well as a large clay jug of water with which to wash away the film of dust from the long journey. This ablution was the final act before putting on the cloak and headdress.

Two women appeared to help with the final adjustments for these garments. They brought a leather pouch with them. As they all began to depart they asked if they could put a special necklace under Adrienne's cloak. The necklace was beautiful and consisted of natural quartz crystals and lapis stones between each crystal, all tied individually with small ties of leather. In the center was the metal circle we had found in Egypt. It had been cleaned and now the nine dots around the circle with one in the center were easily visible. Adrienne was surprised to see the metal charm, and thought.

This had been mine in the life in Egypt when I lived as Shanta. I now know that in my life as Rina this piece was also used in my ritual work.

Dr. Hart had worked with several labs to try and have the unusual combination of metals tested, as one of the metals was unknown. However, the combination had stumped the specialists who had studied the charm so far. While the age of the charm remained undetermined, Adrienne knew it to be a charm that had been in her possession for each of her lives on this planet. It was central to her reincarnations in the universe. As Adrienne's hand touched the charm one more time before she began to walk toward the central site, she put her faith in the outcome of this final circle in the hands of the universal Spirit. Adrienne took a deep, gentle breath, and left the teepee. She was ready, and realized she had been waiting for this moment her entire life, and many other lifetimes before this one as well. It was here they were meant to join again in the circle. Adrienne looked ahead as she walked and could see the circle. All of the people were dressed in light-colored linen. Their gowns were loosely fitted. Some were plain and some were beaded. It was easy to see who had already been wearing such garments more regularly, as opposed to the newly arrived visitors who had very little conscious knowledge of these practices in this lifetime.

As Adrienne approached the circle opened for her. Hands on either side stretched out to reach for her hands. As they joined hands she felt an amazing charge of the most soothing energy. Adrienne felt as though no harm could ever befall her or for that matter, anyone or anything. She felt completely protected. Adrienne looked around at all the people in the circle: Dr. Hart, Asha, Hans, Gina, Ona, Nasha, Meha, Mike and Santee, whom I now recognized as my mother Tiy, from my life as Shanta in Egypt. Each of these people had been with Adrienne in other lifetimes in one way or another. Asha, who held her hand as Shosha in the last circle she participated in, was holding her hand again today.

Seeing this, and the people here, was a testimony to Adrienne that the group would survive, that they would win this final conflict. The last of the fear that Adrienne had held on to finally departed. She felt strong and powerful, a force that could not be defeated.

The chant began. She could hear drums in the background as we began uttering the words Dr. Hart had transcribed. The power Adrienne felt seemed to increase as the group continued to chant. They stood apart from the others, and currents of air began to swirl all around them. The group sang of the world in the beginning, of the beauty inherent in the universe, of the miracle of humanity and of love, of the interconnected aspects of the earth and the creatures therein. The wind swirled around them and even though the wind was loud, Adrienne could hear thunder. She glanced at the sky and, seeing no rain clouds, she realized that the sound that she heard was the sound of horse's hooves. Adrienne looked at Asha first and saw that she was already looking her way. She knew that Adrienne had immediately recalled the memory of the first time we had heard the thunder of horse's hooves at our last circle. She smiled, to remind Adrienne that their destiny was to be quite different during this gathering of the circle. In fact, the world's destiny was to be greatly different, that is, bringing us back to our origins of peace and of love. It was a connection that much of humankind had left behind in history.

Holding hands, the group began to walk slowly around our circle, and thereby creating in fact, a circle of people within a circle that was drawn in the sand. Everyone went very slowly around the fire and the sacred symbols etched in the sand. The group remained very centered and calm in the core of their thoughts. Not even the sand paintings shifted as the breezes blew over them. The group continued the focus of their positive thoughts and the Crystals everyone wore began to glow. A circle of light seemed to emanate from each person, and the glow of those emanations and the crystals began to form a cloud of light around the entire group, almost like a dome. Suddenly, Adrienne could hear the most piercing scream:

"Kill them, every one of them. The girl is mine."

The ground rumbled and seemed to vibrate. The inside of the circle remained a place of calm. Adrienne knew this was their place to be, not just this circle, but the whole world. Somehow her thoughts were linked with the positive thoughts of the others. The group all held their hands tightly, not turning to look at the ugly, violent horde led by the demonic looking leader. This leader, without a doubt, the same creature Adrienne had encountered so many times in the past.

Their thoughts of protection for the world and everyone in it were so powerful that they had created a bubble of energy that covered all within. A ring, or band of light linked each of their crystals together. The light was bright and strong and pulsed with energy. Adrienne felt a slight tug behind her, saw Asha turn slightly, and then straighten back to her original position. Asha's awareness transmitted through all of our thoughts. The group knew the evil horde had arrived. More importantly, they had not been able to break the circle with their weapons. The energy they emulated was negative and dark. The time had arrived, the standoff was final, and this time everyone in the circle was reflecting on the protection of themselves and of the world, having learned that allowing fear to dominate their thinking would allow the negative forces to win. Generations had passed, enough to see that this, the final stand, embraced humanity's hope for a future that was beautiful and bright. This vision was collectively embraced in all the psyches within the circle and to their amazement, an additional eruption of light shot out like a laser and suddenly, the warriors that were trying to kill everyone in the circle, simply disappeared. No trace of them remained. The swirl of dust their horses had generated slowly began to settle. The winds began to diminish. Everyone in the circle was still holding hands so the dome of light and energy remained.

Only as they communicated through their collective thoughts that all were safe, did the energy begin to shift. The bubble of protection now completely faded. The group all stood in complete amazement at all that they had experienced. Everyone began to laugh and hug each other, filled with happiness and relief. As people began to turn and look around they were stunned to see that the dry, parched valley was now lush with green grasses and trees. There was a very large lake and birds flew everywhere. Asha said the energy from the group's combined love and belief in the earth had nourished this land which had been previously abandoned for so long. In the distance everyone could see so many of the tribes celebrating. People were singing and laughing and hugging each other. Dr. Hart, and I looked at each other realizing that all of my dreams and hopes had come true. Hans held my hand as we began to walk toward the tribe's meeting ground. As we walked as a group Adrienne said to everyone, almost thinking aloud

"I don't think I will ever leave this place. There's nothing more I could ever want."

The group all seemed to feel the same way, as they walked toward the others to join the celebration. Adrienne realized that they were starting a tribe of their own. Now that they had witnessed the wonderful miracles that they could create there would be no limit to the things that they could do for themselves, the earth and the universe.

About the Author

MaryKay Duffy has worked for several years as a life and career coach, consultant and author. Her coaching and writing contribute to helping clients as they search for personal clarity, their ideal life and work directions.

MaryKay lives in Massachusetts with her family.

Printed in the United States
900800001B